SIMON SPOTLIGHT
An imprint of Simon & Schuster Children's Publishing Division
1230 Avenue of the Americas, New York, New York 10020

Manufactured in the United States of America

First Edition

2 4 6 8 10 9 7 5 3 1

ISBN 0-689-84542-1

Library of Congress Control Number: 2001090121

Adapted by MARC CERASINI

Based on the screenplay by
JOHN DAVIS
DAVID N. WEISS & J. DAVID STEM
and
STEVE OEDEKERK

From a story by
JOHN DAVIS and STEVE OEDEKERK

Simon Spotlight/Nickelodeon
New York   London   Toronto   Sydney   Singapore

PROLOGUE

A sleek, faster-than-light starship raced through the dark reaches of deep space. Perched at the end of the spaceship's long neck, a command station bustled with activity. Gooey, green creatures flew around in egglike pods.

Unblinking alien eyes monitored the control panels on the ship's high-tech bridge. Suddenly a large central screen began to pulsate.

"Captain! Captain! We have made contact," said the first officer.

The Yokian captain edged the other officers aside. As he moved, green goo sloshed inside his hard, transparent shell. His robotic arms scurried across a control panel as he read the data that was scrolling across the screen.

"Intelligent life?" Captain Spoor asked.

The first officer leaned in close. "I am not sure. Shall we change course and investigate?"

"Of course, you fool!" Captain Spoor replied impatiently. "Great King Goobot demands that we find sacrifices for the Festival of Poultra!"

At the mention of their most sacred god the Yokian crew jumped to their feet.

"Praise Poultra!" they cried. "Beeekaw! Beeekaw! Beeekaw!" Their shells clicked together as they chanted.

"Where is this planet?" the captain asked.

The first officer flew to a navigational controlboard nearby. He tapped a few keys, and an image appeared on the central monitor.

"I have located the solar system," the officer replied. "Nine planets orbiting a central yellow star."

"Change course," Captain Spoor commanded. "We must find these life-forms. Perhaps they will serve as a tasty sacrifice for Poultra."

"Praise Poultra!" the bridge crew cheered.

Slowly the massive chicken-shaped spaceship turned in its orbit and surged ahead toward an unsuspecting green-and-blue planet . . . Earth.

CHAPTER 1

In a remote region of the Colorado desert, far from any town, radar dishes scan the skies over America. The data gathered are fed into computers in a top-secret location deep beneath a rugged mountain range.

Inside the underground control center of the North American Aerospace Defense Command (NORAD), a technician gazed at a large screen.

Suddenly a fast-moving blip appeared on the monitor.

"You better have a look at this, sir."

A burly Air Force commander peered over the technician's shoulder.

"Commercial flight?" he asked.

The technician shook his head. "Too fast, sir."

"One of our own?"

The technician glanced at a computer printout. "The Air Force has nothing scheduled."

The commander's expression was grim. "Then we've got ourselves a bogie."

The commander punched a red button and sirens began to wail. He gave the technician a hard look.

"I don't want this news leaking to the press."

"No, sir!" the technician replied, saluting.

At a nearby Air Force base, fighter pilots scrambled to their jets. Within moments the fighter jets were streaking down the runway.

Once airborne, a pilot's voice crackled over the radio. "Orange Leader to Delta Group. Anticipate visual contact now."

The fighters flew in a tight formation as they sped toward a dark shape in the early-morning skies.

"I can't believe it!" the orange leader cried when he spotted the bogie.

The bogie was a rocket-convertible piloted by a small boy. Behind him sat a nervous-looking chubby kid. And behind that kid was—

"Bark! Bark!"

—a robot dog?!!

"Wow! Nice jets," Jimmy Neutron said as he

waved at the Air Force pilot. "Too bad you guys don't have advanced geothermal-nuclear-thrust capabilities!"

Carl Wheezer swallowed hard and closed his eyes tight as Jimmy yanked the throttle back. The rocket surged forward. Jimmy scanned his control panel.

"Fusion mix stable," he announced. "Cool! We didn't blow up."

Carl opened his eyes. "Whew," he sighed. Then he looked over his shoulder at the jets that were still on their tail. "I think they want us to pull over, Jimmy."

Jimmy shook his head. "We'll have to convene with our aerial brothers at a later date."

He threw a few switches and the rocket took off, leaving the fighter jets far behind.

"Stand by with the satellite!" Jimmy cried.

"Oh . . . okay." Carl fumbled with the toaster-turned-satellite sitting in his lap. "Now . . . what do I do again?"

Jimmy rolled his eyes. "*You* are the deployment system, Carl," he reminded. "As soon as we clear the atmosphere you just . . . throw it!"

"Right," Carl said, still confused.

Jimmy looked down. The ground was getting farther and farther away. He turned to his robot dog.

"Goddard, count down to zero gravity."

Goddard barked, and a side panel in his stomach slid open. A screen lit up with digital numbers as a robotic voice boomed from Goddard's built-in speaker system.

"Zero gravity in T-minus thirty seconds . . . twenty-nine . . . twenty-eight . . ."

"This is it!" Jimmy cried. "Prepare to leave the atmosphere!"

※　　※　　※

In a cozy breakfast nook back on Earth, Jimmy's dad glanced at the morning paper as he sipped hot cocoa.

The headline read: "UFO SIGHTED OVER RETRO-VILLE . . . AIR FORCE DENIES EVERYTHING."

Under the tag line a blurry photo showed the UFO. It looked oddly familiar.

"I had to make the toast in the oven," Mrs. Neutron said, setting a plate in front of her husband. "I can't find our toaster anywhere."

"Well, this oven-toast is brilliant, Sugar Booger!" Mr. Neutron declared. "And these yolks are absolutely perfect too! Run away with me, my love!"

"Okay," Mrs. Neutron replied. "But we'll have to take my car because your transmission needs a compression cuff."

"Whatever," Mr. Neutron said. He dug his hand deep into a cereal box and pulled out the prize.

"Oooh!" he cried happily. "A little duckie! Quack! Quack! Quack!"

"Would you call Jimmy, dear? He's going to be late for school again," said Mrs. Neutron.

"Jimmy! Breakfast!" Mr. Neutron yelled. "Come on down. Quack! Quack!"

There was no reply.

❉ ❉ ❉

Meanwhile, high up in the stratosphere, Jimmy's rocket strained against the tug of Earth's gravity. Carl covered his mouth with his hands, trying to keep his breakfast down.

"UP! UP! UP!" Jimmy cried as the rocket began to slow.

Goddard's digital voice continued the countdown, but got stuck on number nine.

"Engaging pulse rockets now!" Jimmy said, throwing the switch. The engines roared and the rocket sliced upward.

"Just like clockwork," Jimmy noted with pride.

BOOM!

A powerful explosion shook the rocket as the engine began to belch black smoke.

"NOOOO!" Jimmy cried, eyes wide.

"Now?" Carl asked, confused. He tossed the satellite into the air. But since they weren't outside the Earth's gravitational pull yet, it landed back in his lap.

The rocket began a fast descent.

Goddard's digital voice continued the mixed-up countdown.

"11 . . . 15 . . . 45 . . . 290 . . ."

"Jimmy!" cried Carl. "Is this supposed to happen?"

But Jimmy was too busy to reply. "Goddard, Retro-Wrench! Now!"

A mechanical tool rose out of Goddard's metal back and opened like a Swiss Army knife.

Jimmy grabbed the wrench. A light flickered as he tinkered with the control panel.

"I must have underestimated the thrust-to-fuel ratio," Jimmy confessed.

"Estimated?" yelled Carl.

Jimmy shrugged. "It's a long equation, so I rounded off a few numbers."

The rocket spun toward the ground far below. "Think, think, think!" Jimmy repeated to himself.

Carl watched the ground rising up to meet them. "Hurry, Jimmy!" he moaned.

"Quick!" Jimmy cried. "Gimme your lunch!"

Carl paled. "My . . . lunch?"

Jimmy grabbed the lunchbox and dug through it. He tossed Carl's peanut-butter sandwich and his cookies over the side. He pulled out a knitting needle and a ball of yarn. Jimmy looked at Carl, puzzled.

"So, I like to knit," Carl said defensively.

"Ah-ha!" Jimmy cried, holding up a can of soda.

Jimmy stuck out his hand. As if reading Jimmy's mind, Goddard opened his robot mouth and dispensed a line of duct tape. Jimmy shook the soda can, then taped it to the satellite. He tied some loose thread from Carl's shirt to the tab of the can.

Then Jimmy threw the satellite high into the air. As Carl's shirt began to unravel, Jimmy grabbed the thread and pulled hard. The soda can popped open, spewing cola. The pressure from the can lifted the satellite up and up until it flew into orbit.

"Wow!" Carl cried, impressed.

Jimmy winked. "Don't try that at home."

Just then the rocket engine gasped, sputtered, and conked out. The rocket hung in the air for an instant, then dropped like a stone.

The boys looked at each other. "AHHHHH-HHHHHHRRGH!"

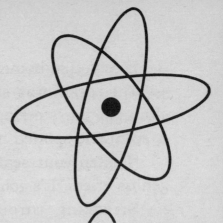

CHAPTER 2

The wind whipped through Jimmy Neutron's hair as he fought to steady the rocket.

"Must . . . engage . . . glide . . . stabilizers . . ."

Jimmy hit the STABILIZER button, and stubby wings popped out of the fuselage. The wings caught the air, but the rocket was still flying out of control. Jimmy tugged at the steering wheel.

"Now a quick stop at my house . . ."

"I don't know," Carl said. "We got to get to school on time. Besides—"

Before Carl could finish his sentence, Jimmy pushed the EJECT button.

"NO!" Carl screamed. "I didn't mean—"

A powerful thruster ignited under Carl's seat. He was blasted up and out of the cockpit.

"Jimmmmmmmyyyy!" Carl screamed.

Then a parachute blossomed above him, and Carl floated away.

"See you in homeroom!" Jimmy called out.

The rocket was still veering wildly. Jimmy clung to the steering wheel as he made his descent. He spotted his house in the distance.

"Fasten your seat belt, Goddard!" the boy genius cried. "It's going to be a bumpy ride."

Streaking through his neighborhood, Jimmy's rocket scraped parked cars, toppled mailboxes, and frightened pets.

By the time it made the final approach to the Neutron home, it was pretty well beat up. The shiny coat of paint was scraped away. The once-sleek fins were twisted and bent. Jimmy's windshield was cracked, and the engine was making loud sputtering noises.

Jimmy pointed the dented nose of his rocket toward his house and readied the air brakes for a soft landing. But when Jimmy yanked the brake control, nothing happened.

"We have brake failure, Goddard!" Jimmy cried. "Brace for impact!"

CRASH! The rocket came to rest against the half-shattered chimney. Jimmy struggled out of the wreckage and dusted himself off.

Goddard's head was spinning.

"Well," Jimmy said. "That wasn't so bad, huh?"

With a loud crash the rest of the chimney fell away.

"James Isaac Neutron!" hollered Mrs. Neutron.

Jimmy ducked down. His mother stood in the front yard, waving a finger at him. Some of the neighbors were peeking out of windows.

"I see you up there!" she said. "How many times have we told you not to land on the roof?"

"Uh . . . probably nine," Jimmy replied sheepishly.

Goddard nodded.

"Exactly nine," Jimmy said. "They say repetition is good for a developing brain."

Mrs. Neutron sighed. "Just what do you think you're doing?"

Jimmy got excited. "Last night I received a message from outer space, but it was garbled in the ionosphere, so I had to launch a communications toaster . . . I mean, satellite . . . and then when I tried—"

"A message from space. Wow!" Mr. Neutron said as he walked over.

Mrs. Neutron shot her husband a look. "Don't encourage him, Hugh."

She turned back to her son. "We have repeatedly told you not to talk to strangers, Jimmy."

"Aw, but Mom," Jimmy whined. "I'm on the verge of contact with an advanced alien civilization!"

Mrs. Neutron shook her head.

"I don't care how advanced they are," she said. "If your father and I haven't met them, they're strangers. Right, Hugh?"

"You are absolutely right, Sugar Booger. Except for policemen," Mr. Neutron said. "He can talk to them, right?"

Jimmy grabbed Goddard and jumped off the roof. Goddard's ears rotated like propellers, setting Jimmy down gently on the grass.

"You gotta admit that is pretty neat, honey!" Mr. Neutron cried.

Mrs. Neutron gave her husband another look.

"But very unsafe. And unsafe is bad," he added quickly.

Jimmy rolled his eyes. "But—"

"No 'buts.' Now, go get ready for school," Jimmy's mom instructed, nudging him along. "Or you'll miss the bus."

CHAPTER 3

Jimmy rushed up the stairs and burst into his room. Instead of posters of rock stars or sports heroes, Jimmy's room was decorated with pictures of Einstein, Galileo, and his other favorite scientists.

A large telescope was set in front of a window. Nearly completed blueprints for future rocket designs were spread across his desk, and models hung from the ceiling.

Jimmy opened his closet door and spoke a command.

"Auto-butler! Activate!"

Hidden panels inside the closet opened to reveal nimble robotic arms. Jimmy stood at the mirror while these mechanical arms fluttered all around him. In seconds they dressed him in his school clothes.

Then Jimmy went into the bathroom, where

lasers stripped the grime from his face and the plaque from his teeth. A warning light blinked and Jimmy closed his eyes. A blast of pressurized water rinsed his face. Then a robotic comb adjusted his hair, carefully sculpting his signature hairdo.

Jimmy plunked down at the computer and printed out his homework. Under the desk, robot arms tied his shoelaces.

From the ceiling an automatic crane lowered Jimmy's backpack onto his shoulders.

Ready for school, Jimmy looked out the window in time to see the bus turning onto his street.

He ran for the door but didn't get far before he tripped and fell. His shoelaces were tied together.

"Better work out that bug," Jimmy muttered as he retied his shoes the old-fashioned way.

"Bye, Goddard!" Jimmy called.

He hit the street just in time to see the school bus vanish around the corner.

"Oh, no! Not again!"

Jimmy pressed a button on his backpack. Instantly a glowing gravity bubble formed around him. When the bubble was complete he began to jump up and down.

Soon Jimmy was bouncing down the street inside the enormous ball. He hopped over cars and fences and cut across lawns.

"Hey, look!" a kid yelled, pointing out the window of the school bus. "Jimmy is using his bubble thing again!"

The other kids gathered to watch. But Cindy Vortex, the smartest girl in school, stayed in her seat. Her nose remained glued to the notebook in her lap. But it was tough to ignore Jimmy Neutron, especially when his big head hovered right outside her open window.

"Nice invention, *Nerd*-tron," Cindy said. "Too bad someone already invented the *bus*."

"Internal combustion is such an old science," Jimmy replied. "Bubble travel is the way of the future!"

But just then Jimmy slammed face-first into a tree. The bubble burst, and he landed with a clang in a trash can.

As the bus drove by, Jimmy Neutron heard the kids laughing. And Cindy Vortex was laughing loudest of all.

"Hello, Jimmy," a voice said from above. Jimmy tumbled out of the trash can and looked up. Carl dangled from a tree, his parachute tangled in the high branches.

"Carl! Allow me," Jimmy said. He pressed a button on his pack, and robotic scissors emerged. With a snip they cut Carl's harness.

"Ooooffff!"

Carl landed on the ground with a thud.

In the distance the boys heard the school bell ring. They were late. Again.

"What a day, huh?" said Carl with a sigh.

Jimmy patted his friend on the back. "Look on the bright side. The worst is behind us."

Carl got up and rubbed his aching backside. "You can say that again!"

CHAPTER 4

Jimmy and Carl sat at their desks in Mrs. Fowl's fifth-grade class. Cindy Vortex stood at the front of the room, giving a presentation. She drew a complicated chart on the blackboard.

"My fossil-to-chromosome ratio clearly demonstrates that female dinosaurs like this Plesiosaurus were the stronger and smarter of their species."

Cindy glanced at her girlfriends. "But really, what else is new?"

Then she motioned toward Jimmy and the other boys. "After class I'll be happy to demonstrate how boy dinosaurs got their butts kicked by girl dinosaurs on a regular basis."

Jimmy Neutron raised his hand.

"Excuse me," he said, "but the mandible crest of this alleged Plesiosaur is actually that of a male Megalasaur, as defined by last week's

World Congress of Paleontologists."

Cindy slammed her fist down on Mrs. Fowl's desk.

"Those findings were inconclusive and you know it, Neutron!" she cried.

Jimmy threw up his arms. "Hello? What is the standard for research on these extra-credit reports?"

"Uh . . . yes . . . well, never mind," Mrs. Fowl stammered. "Let's move along to show-and-tell, shall we?"

Jimmy's friend Sheen carried a small cardboard box to the front of the classroom.

"This is Ultra Lord!" he announced dramatically. "Inside this unlabeled box is Purple-Vengeance Ultra Lord with Power Fists in rare, never-been-seen condition, making it *highly* collectible."

"Never-been-seen, huh?" Cindy scoffed. "How do you know it's even in there?"

"I never thought of that," Sheen said. He opened the top of the box and peeked inside. Sheen smiled in relief, then gasped and slammed the lid.

"Oh, nooooo!" he howled. The class giggled.

"Hey, Jimmy," Carl whispered. "Want to see a frog?" He displayed the drawing he'd been working on.

"That looks great, Carl," said Jimmy.

Carl looked proud. "What are you drawing, Jimmy?"

The boy genius held up a detailed blueprint of a complicated machine.

"It's a fusion reactor," Jimmy said.

Carl scratched his head. "That's nice too, I guess."

"Carl?" Mrs. Fowl called. "Would you please share with us your show-and-tell?"

Carl pulled a strange-looking object from his pocket.

"This is my inhaler," he began. "It provides fast-acting relief of bronchial swelling due to asthma or allergies. One touch of the button and—"

The inhaler squirted right into Carl's eyes.

"Oww! I can't see!" he howled as he ran for the bathroom.

"Thank you, Carl," Mrs. Fowl said. "Next we have Mr. Dean . . . where is Mr. Dean?"

The door burst open and Nick Dean sauntered in, a lollipop dangling from his sneering lips.

"It's Nick!" Cindy said with a sigh.

"Ah, yes, Nick," Mrs. Fowl said. "You are a tad tardy again."

Nick tossed a piece of paper to Mrs. Fowl. "It took me a little while to copy my mom's handwriting for this late note."

The girls' eyes followed Nick as he walked to his desk. On the way he picked up a pencil and handed it to Cindy.

"Did you drop this?"

"Yes . . . I . . . pencil . . . me drop," she stammered.

Then Nick slouched into his seat and took out a sports magazine.

"Mr. Neutron, we eagerly await another one of your interesting show-and-tells," Mrs. Fowl said.

Jimmy straightened in his seat. "As a matter of fact, I brought my latest invention."

He pulled a small device from his backpack. "Behold the Neutron Shrink Ray!"

"Will it work on your big head?" Cindy asked.

"Sure," Jimmy replied. "But first let's test

it on something as vast as outer space, like, say, *your mouth!*"

Jimmy pointed the shrink ray at Cindy and pressed the button. The device hummed and glowed. Then with a burp, a spark, and a puff of smoke, it shorted out.

"Oooooh, save me from the big, bad shrink ray!" Cindy cried in mock terror. "I'm so tiny now . . . just like Jimmy's brain."

The boy genius was puzzled. "I don't understand. It worked this morning."

Just then the bell rang and everyone scattered.

"It's gotta be a programming error," Jimmy said, tossing the device into his backpack as he left the classroom.

ZAP!

The shrink ray blasted Mrs. Fowl. With a surprised squeak, the teacher was shrunk to the size of a toy soldier.

"Oh, m-my," Mrs. Fowl stammered.

Suddenly a huge, slimy worm popped its head out of the apple on Mrs. Fowl's desk. It dropped to the desk and slithered toward the miniature teacher.

Mrs. Fowl backed up. "You don't frighten me, y-y-you ugly beast!" she said. "I teach fifth grade!"

Then Mrs. Fowl pulled a toothpick from a potato plant growing in a glass nearby and raised it above her head like a sword.

CHAPTER 5

Jimmy decided to walk home from school instead of riding the bus. "Did you see the way Miss Cindy Know-it-all Vortex made fun of me?"

"Don't worry about her," Carl said. "She's just jealous. And anyway, some of the greatest inventors of all time started as hopeless failures too."

"Why, thank you, Carl," Jimmy replied. "I feel much better. I think."

Sheen caught up with the boys. As he adjusted his Ultra Lord mask it fell over his eyes, and he walked right into a telephone pole. A colorful poster was tacked to it.

"Hey! Check this out!" Sheen said, eyes wide.

"Wow!" Jimmy cried. "That looks like the coolest amusement park ever!"

"It says we can meet Ultra Lord . . . live!" Sheen's eyes widened even more.

"And look at that," Jimmy pointed. "There's a state-of-the-art, bone-warping gravity ride!"

"I could hang out with Ultra Lord!" Sheen gushed.

"There's even a petting zoo!" said Carl. "Llamas and capybaras . . ."

"Who cares?" Sheen yelled, grabbing Carl's shoulders and shaking him. "It says, *'Meet Ultra Lord . . . LIVE!'*"

"Yeah, but I'm gonna touch a llama," Carl said. "I'm gonna touch a real, live llama!"

"Oh, man," Jimmy said. "Retroland looks so cool. We've got to go to the grand opening tonight!"

Carl's excitement vanished. "My folks won't let me out on a school night."

Sheen gasped. "Neither will mine."

"Pukin' Pluto," said Jimmy. "There's gotta be something we can do. It's the grand opening!"

Nick Dean had overheard the conversation as he glided past on his skateboard. After a dramatic dismount he turned to Jimmy and his friends.

"Sneak out," Nick said simply.

Jimmy blinked. "Huh?"

"You heard me," Nick replied. "Sneak out."

Carl frowned. "But my parents told me—"

"Parents?" Nick cried. "Are you guys gonna be ten forever? What your parents don't know won't hurt them, right?"

"But Nick," said Jimmy, "sneaking out is so . . . so barbaric."

Nick hopped onto his skateboard.

"Whatever, Neutron," he said. "But there's only one opening night, and anybody who matters is gonna be there."

With that, he skated off, balancing along the curb.

"What do you think, Jimmy?" Sheen asked.

"Well, Nick does have a point," Jimmy said thoughtfully.

He began to pace back and forth. "Think, think, think." Soon he was thinking out loud.

"According to the *Newville Journal of Medicine,* monkeys are easily influenced by positive reinforcement, like giving them a banana. And since human and monkey DNA only differ by two percent, the same principle should work on our parents."

"But, Jimmy," Carl said with a frown, "my

dad is highly allergic to bananas."

"It's not the bananas," Jimmy explained. "It's the *principle*. It's called psychology. All we have to do is butter them up!"

Jimmy pulled a lever on his backpack, converting it into a jetpack.

"Give it a try!" he cried as he lifted off. "We'll go to Retroland *tonight!*"

With a fiery blast Jimmy flew away.

"Do you know what he was talking about?" Sheen asked.

Carl thought about it. "I think we're supposed to give our parents buttered bananas."

✺ ✺ ✺

Jimmy's plan was to buy his mom a gift. But not just *any* gift. Something very special would be needed to change her mind.

But as Jimmy flew past the shop windows on Retroville's main street, he discovered that gifts cost money. And the extra-special ones cost lots and lots of money.

A dozen roses cost two months' allowance.

Jimmy knew his mom loved earrings, but diamond ones cost over ten years' allowance! And though Mrs. Neutron was fond of pearls, a pearl necklace would cost even more.

Then Jimmy had an idea. If I can't *buy* a pearl necklace, I'll have to *make* one. And the same thing goes for roses and diamond earrings.

Darting down a side street, Jimmy flew into a crowded seafood restaurant. Seconds later he flew out with an armload of oysters.

As he turned toward home Jimmy zoomed over a passing train long enough to grab a handful of coal.

A quick stop at the neighbor's rose garden, and Jimmy had all the flowers he needed. And not a moment too soon. His jetpack conked out right over his front yard.

Jimmy landed with a thump outside the Neutron garage. Mrs. Neutron stuck her head out from under the hood of Mr. Neutron's car. Her face was smeared with grease, and she clutched a wrench in one dirty hand.

"Jimmy?" she called. "Is that you?"

"Yeah, Mom," Jimmy said over his shoulder as he raced to his clubhouse. "I'll be back in a minute."

Jimmy headed to his clubhouse. To the

untrained eye it looked like an ordinary club-house. But when Jimmy turned the knob on an old radio, the floorboards parted to reveal his top-secret laboratory. Once inside, Jimmy paused long enough to yank a strand of hair from his head. He held it up to an electronic eye. A laser scanned the hair. Then a computerized voice greeted him.

"DNA match confirmed. Welcome, Jimmy."

A clear tube descended over him. Bright blue smoke filled the container. A moment later the smoke was sucked away, and the tube slid back into place.

"Cootie-cleansing complete," the digital voice announced.

"Here, Goddard!" Jimmy called. "Come on, boy."

The robot dog unplugged his tail from the recharging station and ran to his master.

"Hey! Hey!" Jimmy said, holding up an empty soda can. "Look what I brought ya! Your favorite treat—aluminum!"

Goddard sat up and begged.

"You want it? Okay, sit!"

Goddard sat.

"Now, roll over!"

Goddard rolled over.

"Good dog. Now, play dead!"

Jimmy could hear Goddard's computer working as the robot canine considered Jimmy's command.

BOOM!

Jimmy ducked as pieces of Goddard flew everywhere, bouncing off walls and shattering computer monitors and test tubes.

Before the last echo of the blast faded, Goddard had reassembled himself. He wagged his tail and waited for his treat.

"Note to self," Jimmy said, "fix bug in obedience program."

Jimmy tossed the can high into the air.

Goddard stretched his neck five feet up and caught the can in his mouth.

"C'mon, let's check on the experiments."

Jimmy paused at a goldfish bowl. But this goldfish had little, humanlike arms and legs.

"Darwin is evolving nicely," Jimmy noted. Then he moved on to the next experiment.

Inside an empty hamster cage a metal exercise wheel was spinning wildly.

"The invisible hamsters are looking great!"

Jimmy leaned close to his Venus flytrap plant. It snapped its hungry jaws. Jimmy held up three photos. The Venus flytrap ignored the pictures of Sheen and Carl, but snatched the photo of Cindy Vortex, tearing it to pieces.

"The girl-eating plant is developing quite an appetite," Jimmy said with pride.

Finally Jimmy checked his control station. An array of blinking lights and deep-space scanning equipment hummed and buzzed.

"Still no reply from my toaster-satellite," Jimmy said, disappointed. "It's been a whole day. You'd think we might have heard from an alien civilization by now."

Jimmy patted Goddard on the head. "Oh, well, let's go, boy. We've got work to do!"

Jimmy pulled the oysters from his backpack and placed them on a long conveyor belt.

A robot arm lowered itself from the ceiling and pried the oyster shells open. "Say 'Ahhhhhhhh,'" Jimmy said. He shook some sand from his shoe into each oyster and closed the shells tightly.

"In you go!"

One by one Jimmy put the oysters on his microwave-turned-time-accelerator and set the control for ONE YEAR LATER.

The time accelerator hummed as the clock spun around and around. *DING!* The oysters popped open to reveal glistening, white pearls.

Next Jimmy went to his hydraulic press and dumped lumps of coal into it. A moment later sparkling diamonds tumbled out.

Jimmy inspected the goods. Surely my mom won't be able to resist such treasures, he thought.

CHAPTER 6

"Jimmy!" Mrs. Neutron called. "Where are you?"

Behind her, Jimmy and Goddard emerged from their secret elevator inside the fireplace.

"Hi, Mom!" Jimmy called.

Mrs. Neutron jumped onto the couch, startled. "You scared the bejeebers out of me!"

"Sorry about your bejeebers, Mom. And might I add how lovely you look today."

Mrs. Neutron wiped her face. "Jimmy, I'm covered in transmission fluid."

"Yes," Jimmy replied. "Quite becoming. It's very fashion-forward."

Mrs. Neutron frowned. "What's this about?"

Jimmy pulled a bouquet of roses from behind his back.

"Happy birthday, Mom!"

Mrs. Neutron looked surprised. "These are beautiful! But, sweetie, it's not my birthday."

"It's not?" Jimmy said. "Then whatever will I do with this priceless pearl necklace and these diamond earrings?"

"These can't be real!" Mrs. Neutron cried.

"Oh, but they *can,* and they *are!*"

Jimmy snapped his fingers. Spotlights shined from Goddard's eyes, and game-show music played from his speaker-ears.

"All of these fabulous gifts could be yours," Jimmy said in an announcer's voice. "*If* you know the correct answer to this simple question."

Goddard provided a drumroll.

"*Please,*" Jimmy said in a pleading voice, "can I go to Retroland tonight?"

"Nope," Mrs. Neutron said, handing back the gifts. "It's a school night."

Jimmy couldn't believe his ears.

"Did you just say no?"

Mrs. Neutron nodded.

"But . . . but all my friends are going!" Jimmy cried. "And anybody who matters is going to be there!"

"I matter," Mrs. Neutron said. "Your father matters. And you matter. But you're not going."

"Wait!" Jimmy said, fishing through his

backpack. "I'm sure there must be something in here to change your mind."

Jimmy accidentally pressed the START button, and his rocket-pack ignited.

"Be careful, Jimmy!" Mrs. Neutron ducked as Jimmy flew over her head.

"Holy Moon Pie!" yelled Jimmy.

He flew around the room in uncontrollable circles, knocking down lamps and crashing into furniture. Then Jimmy bounced off the wall and became tangled in the curtains.

WHOOSH! The curtains caught on fire.

"Emergency! Emergency!" Jimmy screamed.

Mrs. Neutron beat the flames with the bouquet of roses, scattering petals all over the living room.

"Must . . . deactivate . . . rocket," Jimmy gasped, struggling against the runaway backpack. Finally he reached the button, cutting the fuel to the rocket engine.

With a crash Jimmy landed on the floor. He grabbed Goddard and aimed him—tail first—at the blazing curtains.

"Goddard, activate extinguisher!" cried Jimmy.

Fireproof foam gushed out of Goddard's back-side, dousing the flames and soaking Mrs. Neutron.

"Okay, Jimmy, that's the last straw," Mrs. Neutron said in a too-calm-to-be-true voice. "We have warned you time and time again about playing with rockets in the house."

"But, Mom!" Jimmy cried. "Technically it's *not* a rocket. It's a jetpack."

"Up to your room, mister!" Mrs. Neutron yelled. "March!"

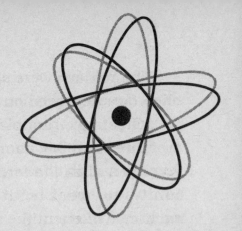

CHAPTER 7

Deep in space Jimmy's toaster-satellite beamed its message into the cosmos.

A rubber-chickenlike starship dropped out of hyperspace, followed by many others. The command ship approached the satellite. Doors opened on the ship's belly, and a beam of light bathed it in an eerie glow.

Seconds later the satellite was sucked into the large craft.

In the hangar of the Yokian command ship the first officer cautiously approached the beeping toaster. As he lifted the device with his robotic hands a slice of toast popped out.

"Captain, we have secured the alien probe."

"Excellent!" Captain Spoor said. He watched as technicians attached a translation device and a large visual monitor. Soon the satellite began to make a high-pitched noise.

The Yokians were shocked when a horrible, alien face appeared on their monitors.

"Greetings from planet Earth!" the hideous creature said. "My name is Jimmy Neutron and you're an alien life-form! I welcome the opportunity to meet with you for the mutual exchange of scientific knowledge and universal brotherhood."

A metal robot barked in the background.

"This is my dog, Goddard . . ."

Captain Spoor leaned closer.

"And these are my parents," Jimmy continued. He held up a photo of his mom and dad.

Captain Spoor's big eyes blinked behind his transparent shell. He leaped to his feet so quickly that green goo sloshed inside of his egg-like body.

"Freeze that image!" he commanded.

The captain studied the picture of Jimmy's parents.

"These large aliens look edible," the captain declared, pointing to Jimmy's parents. "Send word to His Majesty. The search is over!"

The Yokian crew began to chant. "Beeekaw! Beeekaw! Beeekaw!"

❧   ❧   ❧

Back at the Neutron home Jimmy was still pleading his case.

"But, Dad! All my friends are going to be there," Jimmy begged.

"I know, son," Mr. Neutron replied. "But if all your friends were named Cliff, would you jump off them? I don't think you would." He put his arm around his son's shoulder. "Jim, James, Jimmy, Jimbo, Jim, James," he said. "Let me tell you a little about rockets. They're *big*-people things, son. And you just can't go around playing with flying, fiery, big-people things. Because that's what rockets are. Rockets are flying things."

Mr. Neutron rose. "Well, I hope this talk has helped. Oh, and by the way, Mom said you're grounded. Sorry!"

After his father had left, Jimmy slumped on his bed. "What good is it to be a ten-year-old genius if you can't even go out on a school night?" Jimmy toyed with his rubber goo darts. "Goddard . . . I need options."

Goddard's computer screen flipped open.

Jimmy read: APOLOGIZE. YOUR PARENTS LOVE YOU.

"Nope. Next," Jimmy said. He lobbed a goo dart at the screen.

CREATE A TIME CAPSULE. ESCAPE TO THE FUTURE.

Another goo dart hit the screen with a slap.

"Takes too long," said Jimmy. "Next!"

SNEAK OUT.

"Hmm . . . that sounds familiar," Jimmy said. "That's it! Barbaric problems call for barbaric solutions. Phone, please."

Goddard's ear flew off in Jimmy's direction. Jimmy snatched the ear-phone and dialed.

"Hello, Carl? It's me. Tell Sheen to meet us at Retroland in one hour . . . we're sneaking out!"

CHAPTER 8

Upstairs in his room Jimmy made a few last-minute adjustments to his shrink-ray gun.

"Okay, Goddard, you know what to do?"

Goddard barked once then jumped under the blankets on Jimmy's bed.

"Good boy!"

Jimmy aimed the shrink ray at himself.

ZAP!

Instantly Jimmy shrank to the size of an action figure.

"See you later, Goddard," the tiny figure squeaked. Jimmy lifted the now gigantic shrink ray and stumbled into the hall. But then he lost his balance, and the device bounced down the steps and landed on the couch between his mom and dad.

"Jimmy's a big boy now," Mr. Neutron was saying. "Don't worry about him, Sugar Booger."

Mrs. Neutron sighed. "Oh, I suppose you're right."

"I was a kid once," Mr. Neutron said. "I remember being grounded a whole week and not being able to go to my best friend's bachelor party."

Mr. Neutron reached for his television remote but grabbed the shrink ray instead.

Mrs. Neutron turned to her husband. "Well, what did you do?"

Without looking, Mr. Neutron pressed a button and shrank the television. Then he hit the button again, and the television sprang back to normal size.

"Well, actually, I snuck out," Mr. Neutron confessed.

"Hugh! You don't think that Jimmy . . ."

Mr. Neutron dropped the shrink ray onto the floor. Jimmy crawled along the living-room floor, trying to reach it.

"Oh, no, no!" Mr. Neutron said, patting his wife's hand. "It's not like he can just walk right out the front door!"

Mr. Neutron crossed his legs just as Jimmy grabbed the shrink ray. His dad kicked the tiny boy clutching the shrink ray into the air and right through the mail slot in the front door.

Jimmy bounced down the steps, the shrink ray zapping things right and left and eventually zapping Jimmy back to his normal size.

"And I thought my regular size was small!" Jimmy muttered as he took off for Retroland.

◆ ◆ ◆

Cindy Vortex was in her room practicing Tai Chi moves while she ate a frozen Purple Flurp bar. Her best friend, Libby, looked up from her homework.

"Tell me what you're supposed to be doing again?" Libby said.

"Tai Chi promotes wellness, and relaxes and energizes the body," Cindy explained. "Whereas Purple Flurp, being ninety-eight percent sugar, creates tension and a temporary rush of energy. I figure if I do them together, I can achieve perfect balance."

Libby put down her book.

"Cindy? Do you think you'll ever get married?"

"What?! To a boy?! Are you crazy?"

Libby sat up. "C'mon, boys aren't that bad."

"What are you talking about!" cried Cindy. "They're stubborn, grimy, noisy, and completely disgusting. *And* they only have *one* thing on their minds . . ."

"Belching!" Libby replied.

Cindy shook her head. "A boy? No, thank you."

"Not all boys are like that," Libby insisted. "I mean, you do kind of like Nick Dean, right?"

Cindy giggled. "What? I . . . well, he is kind of . . . oh, I do not!"

❈ ❈ ❈

Inside Jimmy's underground laboratory the long-range Space Scanner began to beep.

A message scrolled across the monitor: WARNING! UNIDENTIFIED FLYING OBJECTS DETECTED . . .

Hundreds of moving objects filled the screen, approaching planet Earth.

CHAPTER 9

Jimmy and his friends met at the entrance to Retroland.

Sheen wore his favorite Ultra Lord mask. Carl wore a T-shirt that said I LOVE LLAMAS.

"Wow! It's even better than the poster!" Jimmy said. He threw his arms over his friends' shoulders. "Gentlemen," he said, "this will be a night we shan't easily forget."

The boys hopped on the Eye-in-the-Sky cable-car ride first. They sat inside a gigantic eyeball that floated high over the park.

"Eye-mazing!" Sheen declared. "Let's find the Octapuke!"

Moments later they were engulfed in the Octapuke's mechanical tentacles, twirling around and around. Carl's face turned red and then white.

Jimmy cocked his head and looked at Carl,

who had turned green. "I believe Carl is experiencing vertigo so severe it's causing digestive spasms," he noted.

Sheen blinked, confused. "What does that mean, Jimmy?"

"To put it simply, he's gonna barf."

After they helped Carl out of his seat, the boys spotted Nick Dean. He was in the tattoo tent, getting a smiley skull put on his arm. Girls swooned around him. When he saw them, Nick nodded and gave Jimmy the thumbs-up.

The boys were on their way to the Show-Me-the-Mummy ride when Sheen stopped short and began to stammer. "It's . . . It's . . . It's—"

"Some guy dressed up like Ultra Lord," said Jimmy.

"No!" Sheen cried. "It *is* Ultra Lord. I'd recognize him anywhere!"

Sheen's gaze followed Ultra Lord as he strode through the crowd. Suddenly the boy was face-to-face with his hero.

"Mighty Ultra Lord, it's . . . it's truly an honor!" Sheen gasped.

Ultra Lord posed for a picture with Sheen then put his hand on the boy's shoulder.

"Do you promise to use your powers for good and not evil?" Ultra Lord asked in a booming voice.

"Yes! Yes, Ultra Lord," Sheen promised.

"Now, counterpart," said Ultra Lord, "you may lead the fight for justice!"

Sheen was so excited, he fainted in his hero's arms.

"Uh . . . is this kid with anybody?" asked the man inside the Ultra Lord costume.

At the petting zoo Carl edged toward the llama ring. Cautiously he reached out a hand and touched the llama.

"Whoa!!!!" he cried. "This is so cool!"

The boys paused in front of the Bat-out-of-Heck ride. An evil, gaping mouth stared back at them. Inside they could hear people screaming.

"Now, that's what I call a ride!" Sheen cried.

As the boys rushed to the gate, Jimmy was stopped by the attendant. The man made Jimmy stand next to a sign that read: YOU MUST BE THIS TALL TO RIDE.

Jimmy just made it. Then the attendant squashed Jimmy's hair down.

"Sorry, pal," the attendant said. "Hair don't count. Them's the rules."

Jimmy raised a finger. "Excuse me for a moment."

He raced around a corner and pulled the shrink ray gun out of his pocket. Jimmy flicked a switch marked REVERSE, then pulled the trigger. There was a loud *ZAP* and a flash of light. When Jimmy returned he was gigantic.

"Wow!" the attendant cried. "They sure grow up fast!"

On the Bat-out-of-Heck ride the boys caught up with Nick Dean.

"This ride is beyond awesome!" Sheen cried.

Nick chuckled. "Yeah, just think, if you had listened to your parents, you'd be home in bed instead of riding this monster!"

As the coaster plunged down a very steep hill Nick threw his hands into the air. Jimmy and his friends did too.

✹ ✹ ✹

Later that night Mr. and Mrs. Neutron decided to check on their son.

"I told you," Mr. Neutron insisted, "he's fine."

"Just a quick peek, Hugh," Mrs. Neutron whispered.

She pushed the door open and peeked in. Jimmy's bedroom was dark, but they could see a lump under the blanket.

"There, now what did I tell ya?" Jimmy's dad said.

"Jimmy?" Mrs. Neutron called. "Are you awake?"

Under the blanket Goddard activated his Jimmy-voice circuits. "Yes, Mother. I am awake."

"Son," Mr. Neutron said, "your mother and I just wanted to say good night."

"Yes," Mrs. Neutron added, "and to tell you that we love you."

Mrs. Neutron tried to pull the covers back for a good-night kiss, but Goddard held on tight.

"Oh, honey. I know you're upset. And we don't like to punish you. You're such a special boy. Maybe we can go to Retroland next weekend, Jimmy," Mrs. Neutron said.

Goddard was silent.

Mrs. Neutron sighed as she left the room.

"See you in the morning, son," Mr. Neutron said as he closed the door behind him.

In the blackness of space the Yokian chicken-ships moved into Earth's orbit. Flames spewed from their engines as they thundered toward the planet below.

On the bridge of the command ship an image of the Yokian king and his henchman, Ooblar, appeared on a huge viewscreen.

"Attention all Yokians," Ooblar said. "His esteemed Majesty, king Goobot, will now speak. Goon Gak Poo!"

The captain bowed as he and his crew repeated the royal greeting.

"Goon Gak Poo! Goon Gak Poo!"

King Goobot waved his hand.

"Yes, yes, yes, very nice," he said. "Thank you all so much."

Then King Goobot noticed that one crew member had not saluted him.

"You there! Why have you not Goon Gak Pooed me?"

"Huh? What?" the confused crewman replied.

King Goobot frowned. "Space him."

The Yokian screamed and struggled, but it

was no use. A moment later he was blown out of the airlock and into space.

"So, captain, tell me good news," King Goobot commanded.

"My king," Captain Spoor began. "We have entered Earth's orbit. Scans reveal the planet to be populated with a variety of fleshy bipeds."

"Ahhhhh," the king sighed. "Poultra's favorite."

"Praise Poultra!" Ooblar cried.

The crew jumped to their feet.

"Beeekaw! Beeekaw! Beeekaw!"

King Goobot silenced the crew with a wave of his hand. "I do hereby proclaim—"

"Proclaim with full vigor, O great, sloshy one!" Ooblar cried.

The king scowled at Ooblar.

"I do hereby proclaim that I grant permission to commence with the commencing!"

"The commencing shall commence!" Ooblar shouted. "All hail the commencer, for he alone does the commencing!"

"Ooblar . . ."

"I'm sorry, sir," Ooblar said as he slinked away.

"Waste no time, captain," the king said. "The

festival grows near. And remember, only the large specimens will do. Size *does* matter."

The chicken-ships pointed their beaks toward the green-and-blue planet below and began their final descent.

CHAPTER 10

Later that night Mrs. Neutron lay on her bed reading her book, *Unwrapping the Gifted Child*. Mr. Neutron kept interrupting her.

"Here comes Mr. walky man, Mr. walky, Mr. walky, walky man," he said as he walked his fingers up and down her arm. "My, what nice elbows you have."

Mrs. Neutron looked up from her book. "According to this," she said, "we should encourage Jimmy without overindulging him."

"Okay!" Mr. Neutron replied. "What does it say about rockets?"

Just then they heard a strange noise from downstairs.

"Is someone in the kitchen?" Mrs. Neutron asked nervously.

"The kitchen? Uh . . . I didn't hear anything."

Mrs. Neutron pointed toward the door.

Reluctantly Mr. Neutron crept downstairs.

The living room was dark, but there was something moving in the kitchen.

"Jimmy?"

Mr. Neutron peeked around the corner. Suddenly he was bathed in an eerie green light.

"You're not Jimmy!" Mr. Neutron cried.

There was a whirring sound and a bright flash. Mr. Neutron screamed. Then all was quiet.

"Hugh? Are you all right?" Mrs. Neutron called, rushing down the steps.

There was a second bright flash. Mr. and Mrs. Neutron floated out of their house on the beam of light, as if in a trance. All over the neighborhood, beams rained down from space. And every grown-up of Retroville was sucked into the spaceships hovering above.

When the last of Retroville's adult population was aboard, the chicken-ships streaked across the sky and disappeared into space.

🐔 🐔 🐔

Jimmy and his friends walked home from Retroland.

"That was great!" Jimmy cried.

"Mindbending," Sheen agreed. "You know, Nick is not such a bad guy," said Sheen.

"He's a *genius!*" said Carl. "No offense, Jimmy."

"None taken," Jimmy Neutron replied. "Actually, I find Nick's insights on how to deal with one's parents quite refreshing."

"Wouldn't it be great if our folks all just disappeared for a while?" Sheen said.

"Yeah," Jimmy agreed. "That way we could do whatever we wanted, whenever we wanted. We'd be free!"

"Sounds nice," Carl sighed. He looked up. "Hey, look at that big shooting star!"

"Cool," Sheen said. "You get to make a wish."

"I know what I'd wish for," Jimmy declared. "I'd wish for no more parents!"

✺ ✺ ✺

The next morning Jimmy's tiny rocket-ship alarm clock smoldered on its launchpad next to his bed. A digital voice began a countdown.

"Liftoff in five seconds . . . in four . . . three . . . two . . . one . . ."

With a rumble the miniature rocket lifted off. Attached to the rocket was a long string which pulled the blankets off a sleeping Jimmy and rolled him out of bed.

Jimmy sprang to his feet, rubbing the sleep out of his eyes. "Abort mission!" he mumbled.

The rocket crashed into the wall and dropped to the floor. Jimmy turned to Goddard.

"Wake mode!" he cried. The robot dog powered up and his lights went on.

"Come on, boy! I'll race ya to the kitchen."

"Bark! Bark!" Goddard bounced down the steps on springy legs.

"Hey, Mom?" Jimmy called. "Did you get any more Purple Flurp bars?"

There was no reply. "Mom?"

Jimmy noticed a note taped to the refrigerator:

DEAR SON/DAUGHTER,
WE WENT TO FLORIDA FOR AN EXTENDED
VACATION.

LOVE, YOUR PARENTS

All over town the kids of Retroville were reading the same note.

Carl and Sheen burst into Jimmy's kitchen just as Jimmy was taking down the note.

"My mom and dad went to Florida on vacation," Jimmy said.

"Yeah," Sheen replied. "Our parents went to Florida too."

Jimmy and his friends went outside. Everywhere they looked, kids wandered around confused.

"From the look of it, I'd say a lot of parents have gone away," Jimmy guessed.

"Did they all go to Florida?" Carl asked.

"Maybe they went to get orange juice or something," Sheen said.

"I don't digest pulp well," Carl sighed.

Jimmy tapped Goddard. "Scan for adult lifeforms," he commanded.

A scanning dish popped out of Goddard's back and began to rotate. Jimmy read the data that Goddard gathered on his computer screen.

"Just as I thought," he said. "There are no grown-ups anywhere within radar range. They're all gone. The whole town—no parents."

"No parents?" Carl said solemnly.

Sheen scratched his head.

Then it hit them.

"No PARENTS!!!" they cried.

CHAPTER 11

The town of Retroville turned into a rule-free kid paradise. It became a giant theme park that was bigger than Retroland itself—and even better.

Jimmy and his friends headed downtown. At the entrance to the shopping mall a girl stopped the boys.

"The escalators are for handrail riding only." she informed them. "And no hands, please!"

"Wheeeee!" Sheen cried as he slid down.

All the game arcades were free, thanks to a little tampering by Nick Dean. Sheen ran up a tally of 900,000,000 points on the Ultra Lord Challenge. It was his best score ever!

At the arcade Jimmy and Carl lost sight of Sheen. They found him an hour later at Toys and Stuff. He was clutching boxes of Ultra Lord action figures, mostly the hard-to-find Red Riot version with Firing Fists and Fighting Feet.

Greetings from Earth! My name is Jimmy Neutron!

Goddard, brace for impact!

What good is it being a ten-year-old genius if you can't even go out on a school night?

SNEAK OUT!

Every grown-up in Retroville is sucked into the spaceships hovering above.

Goddard, the Earth's been visited by aliens!

Let's go get our parents!

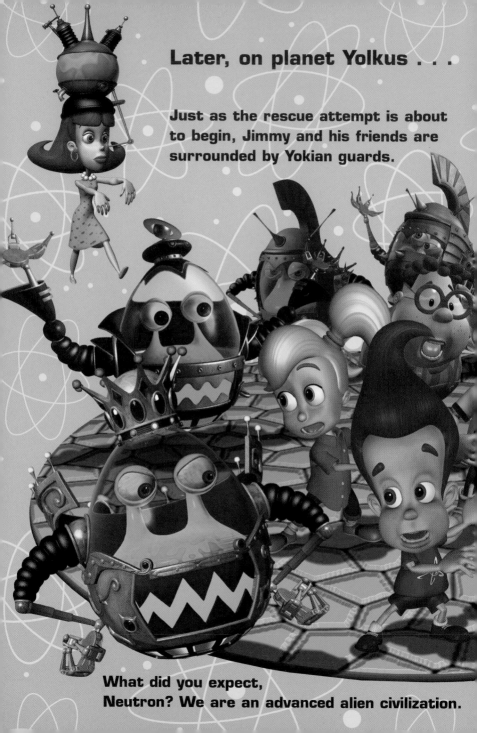

Later, on planet Yolkus . . .

Just as the rescue attempt is about to begin, Jimmy and his friends are surrounded by Yokian guards.

What did you expect, Neutron? We are an advanced alien civilization.

Goddard, play dead!

Finally, everything is back
to normal in Retroville.
For now . . .

"I'm not going! I'm not going!" he screamed as Jimmy and Carl dragged him away.

"Come on," Carl insisted. "Let's go have lunch."

At the Bun 'n' Burger the grill was sizzling. Hamburgers were free, and there were no lettuce and tomatoes to spoil the taste. All orders were supersize only, and the customers were each given their own pitcher of soda.

"I've always wondered what a chocolate milkshake with soda would taste like," Carl said, smacking his lips.

The Candy Bar soda shop was turned into a dancehall and food-fight arena. Carl had a chocolate-syrup-chugging contest with Nick Dean. Carl won. But then Nick Dean lobbed a cherry pie at him.

Soon the boys were covered with whipped cream and Carl's favorite—cherry filling.

"How are we going to get this stuff off?" Sheen asked as he licked his fingers clean.

"Follow me!" Jimmy replied.

He led them to the Retroville fire station, which had been transformed into a water park.

"Whoa!" said Jimmy as a high-pressure water hose blasted him clean.

Behind the firehouse the rescue nets became trampolines. "This is more fun than my transportation bubble!" gushed Jimmy.

"I'm flying! Just like Ultra Lord!" Sheen cried as he bounced higher and higher.

Goddard bit the tops off of all the fire hydrants, flooding the town.

Cindy Vortex waved as she jet-skied past the firehouse. Libby was right behind her.

All over town kids left the lights on and the refrigerator doors open. They entered through the exits, went up the down staircases, and swung from the light fixtures. They played their music really loud, sat too close to the TVs, and jumped on the furniture.

On the way to the homework bonfire Jimmy and his friends stopped at the petting zoo where animals roamed around freely.

"I'm gonna touch the llama!" Carl said.

"Touch it?" Jimmy replied. "You can *ride* it if you want to!"

As night fell, the kids gathered around a bonfire outside the elementary school. There were hotdogs-on-a-stick, roasted marshmallows, and S'mores. A rock band played long into the night.

Jimmy, Carl, and Sheen ate and danced and ate some more. They stayed up way past their bedtimes until they could hardly keep their eyes open.

With the fire crackling, their stomachs stuffed, and the stars overhead, they all agreed that Florida was the very best place for their parents to be!

CHAPTER 12

The armada of Yokian chicken-ships dropped out of space and went into orbit around their highly industrialized planet.

The surface of planet Yolkus was covered with glass-and-steel cities and mile-high skyscrapers. From orbit, lights from the buildings rivaled the glow of the nearby sun.

Inside the royal palace of Yolkus, King Goobot was bored. He gazed down at his subjects from his high throne, his bulging eyes sleepy. Then he sloshed back in his shell and settled in for a nap.

Ooblar suddenly appeared beside his throne.

"Captain Spoor has arrived, O distinguished, squishy leader."

The king perked up instantly. "Oh, goody! Oh, goody! At last! Send him in."

A massive door swung open and Captain

Spoor entered with his first officer.

"Goon Gak Poo!" Captain Spoor saluted.

"Oh, Poo to you too," King Goobot replied with a dismissive wave. "Now, what have you brought me?"

"We have a fine crop for your inspection," said the captain. "And the Hats of Obedience have been implanted, my king." He turned to the first officer. "Display the harvest!"

"Aye, aye, sir!" The first officer toggled the remote control he held in his robot hands. Like zombies on parade, the parents of Retroville marched into the room. They stared straight ahead, hypnotized. Each wore a strange-looking hat with a red, blinking light that crackled with electricity—the Hat of Obedience.

The first officer flicked the control forward and the humans bowed in unison.

"Oooh! Gimme, gimme!" cried King Goobot. "I wanna play! I wanna play!"

The king snatched the remote control and twisted the joystick.

Mr. Neutron stepped forward and raised his arm.

Delighted, King Goobot moved the stick

again. This time Mr. Neutron shimmied and shook.

Soon the king had Mr. Neutron strutting around and mouthing words like a ventriloquist's dummy.

"Hel-lo, I am a stu-pid Earth man," Mr. Neutron was made to say. "I am ve-ry stu-pid. Stu-pid, stu-pid, stu-pid. I have a lit-tle ti-ny brain . . ."

King Goobot laughed. "I love this! Now, watch."

The king made Mr. Neutron slap himself in the face again and again.

"Why are you hitting yourself, Earth man?" the king asked with a cruel chuckle.

Suddenly the light on Mr. Neutron's hat blinked from red to green. The human twitched, then spoke. "Hi, Sugar Booger, you look good enough to eat today!"

Mr. Neutron hopped onto King Goobot's lap and gave him a big kiss.

Outraged, the king sputtered and threw the remote control. The device bounced across the floor and Mr. Neutron's headset blinked back to red. He jerked to zombielike attention.

"I will not tolerate this insolence. Have this creature destroyed immediately!" King Goobot cried.

The Yokian officer stepped forward. "My king, if I may? . . ."

He picked up the remote. "It is merely a glitch of the control device . . ."

The first officer toggled the joystick, and Mr. Neutron's light blinked green again. He waved and blew a kiss.

"You see?" the first officer continued. "When the device is manipulated too aggressively, certain random impulses—"

"Are you saying it's my fault?" King Goobot demanded.

The first officer cowered in his shell. "No, Your Majesty!" he cried. "I was merely explaining why—"

King Goobot turned to Ooblar and held out his hand. "Doomstick."

Ooblar handed King Goobot a long wand. The king waved it once then touched the first officer's shell. The Yokian vanished in a puff of fluorescent green smoke.

"Anyone else think it was my fault?" King

Goobot asked. "No? Okay, then."

He tossed the Doomstick aside.

"Take these Earth vermin to the processing plant for purification," King Goobot said mischievously. "Make sure they are prepared for *the Festival!*"

CHAPTER 13

Jimmy Neutron woke up to the sound of Goddard whimpering. Slowly the boy genius opened his eyes.

He found himself lying on the grass in front of the school. Jimmy smelled smoke from the smoldering ashes that had once been a giant bonfire. He heard strange sounds all around him.

Jimmy sat up. Hundreds of kids were sprawled in the grass, groaning.

"Morning, Goddard," Jimmy said softly as he rubbed his aching head. "What a night."

Jimmy heard a voice cry out.

It was Carl. He was lying in the grass nearby, muttering in his sleep.

"Oh, I'm stuffed now," he moaned. "I couldn't have another . . . well, okay, one more. I'm gonna have one more and that'll be it. . . ."

Sheen stuck his head out of the bushes.

"Are there any survivors?"

Jimmy stumbled to his feet. Through bleary eyes Jimmy saw Nick Dean slouched against a tree, unaffected.

"Shake it off, Neutron," Nick said.

Jimmy shook his head. "Oww!"

"I gotta get home," he said. "Mom and Dad might be back by now. Come on, Goddard!"

Jimmy and his dog hurried down Retroville's main street. It was like a ghost town. Candy wrappers and empty snack boxes lay strewn across the sidewalk. Store windows were broken, and the fire hydrants all leaked water.

Jimmy waved his finger at Goddard. "Bad dog!" he scolded.

As they passed the electronics store a television displayed in the window caught Jimmy's attention.

"We interrupt this program to bring you this special report," said the news-anchor boy.

"Trouble in paradise. That's what some kids are saying in the aftermath of yesterday's 'No Parents' celebrations."

The cameras turned to Courtney Taylor, reporter-girl.

"What started as an awesome day has become, like, a real bummer," she said. Courtney thrust the microphone under the nose of a sobbing boy.

"I was playing on the teeter-totter," he said. "And the next thing I knew, I was on the ground and my knee was hurt."

The camera switched back to Courtney Taylor. "Reports of tummy aches, owies, and constipation have reached epidemic numbers over the past few hours, with little indication of slowing down."

A little girl with a huge bloated stomach appeared on the television screen. "We were gonna see who could eat the most cotton candy," the girl moaned. "And I won! . . ."

Clutching her stomach, the little girl began to wail. "I want my mommy!"

"So, there you have it," said Courtney. Then her lip began to quiver, and tears ran down her cheeks. "I want my mommy too!" she bawled.

Jimmy Neutron got the feeling that something was rotten in Retroville. He raced home as fast as he could.

"Mom? Dad?" Jimmy called. He searched the

whole house and found it empty.

"What kind of parents take off and leave their kid all alone?"

He plopped down on his bed. "And they didn't even say good-bye."

Goddard's head spun once. Then a holographic projector popped out of his back. A 3-D image of Jimmy's mom and dad appeared. It was footage taken the night Jimmy snuck out.

"Son," the projection of Mr. Neutron said, "your mother and I just wanted to say good night."

"Yes," the hologram of his mom said, "and to tell you that we love you."

Goddard wagged his tail and hit the FAST-FORWARD button. He slowed the recording near the end.

"Maybe we can go to Retroland next weekend, Jimmy," the 3-D Mrs. Neutron said.

"Can my fabulous dog come too?" Goddard asked in Jimmy's voice.

"Sure," Mr. Neutron said. "Goddard can come too. See you in the morning, son."

"Sweet dreams," his mom said softly.

Jimmy sighed and sniffed back a tear.

"Okay," he sighed. "So they said good night."

Then Jimmy jumped to his feet.

"Hey, wait a minute!" he cried. "Play back that last part again. Audio only."

Goddard barked and activated the sound.

"See you in the morning, son."

"In the morning?!" Jimmy repeated. "Why would he say that if they weren't going to *be* here?"

Jimmy pulled out the note his parents left him. Now he was sure something was wrong.

"Come on, Goddard," Jimmy said. "Let's go to the lab!"

Jimmy ran the note through his handwriting-analysis machine. He studied the image carefully.

"Just as I suspected," he said. "This note is a fake!"

Goddard began to bark.

"What is it, boy?"

Goddard scampered over to the long-range Space Scanner. On the control panel a red light flashed a warning.

"The scanner has detected something!" Jimmy cried. "Jumpin' Jupiter! Something has entered Earth's atmosphere from deep space!"

Jimmy adjusted some dials.

"Look!" he gasped. "It's an ion signature!"

Jimmy paced back and forth as he reviewed the facts out loud.

"Let's see," he said. "The long-range Space Scanner detected an ion signature in the Earth's atmosphere. What could it be? There was that bright shooting star that we saw. Could it have been something else?"

Jimmy stopped pacing and rubbed his chin. "Now all the grown-ups are missing. The note says they went to Florida, but the note is an obvious fake . . ."

Jimmy began to pace again. "Think, think, think!"

Then he froze in his tracks. "Could my satellite have been detected—by aliens?!"

CHAPTER 14

Carl dropped his comic book and stared at Jimmy.

"Okay, so you're saying that our parents have been kidnapped by aliens? And that me, you, and a metal dog are going to battle an alien civilization?"

Jimmy rubbed Goddard's head.

"Oh, but you're a good metal dog! Aren't you, boy?"

"Bark! Bark!"

Jimmy peeked under the engine panel of his rocket. Tools were scattered all over the yard.

Carl glanced up nervously. "You know, the last time we tried this we couldn't even break free of the atmosphere."

"I know," Jimmy replied with a wave of his hand. "But I recalculated the thrust-to-fuel ratio and I've adjusted the engine accordingly."

KLUNK! Carl jumped backward as the engine dropped out of the rocket and landed on the driveway.

"I can fix that!" Jimmy assured his friend.

Suddenly a mob of kids charged into the yard yelling for Jimmy.——

"Neutron!" Nick Dean cried. "Hey, big head! Where are you?"

Jimmy ran and hid behind his clubhouse. Carl was right behind him.

"What's going on?" Carl asked in a shaky voice.

"An angry mob," Jimmy replied. "In times of crisis, intellectuals are always the first to go!"

Carl peeked around the clubhouse. "Well, they don't *look* angry. They look like they're about to barf."

Jimmy peered over Carl's head. Then he took a deep breath and stepped forward.

When the kids saw him, the crowd parted and Nick Dean emerged, gripping a struggling Sheen with one hand.

"You are messing with powers far beyond your mortal comprehension," Sheen said in a fair imitation of Ultra Lord's voice.

"Okay, Neutron," Nick said, still holding Sheen. "Ultra Freak here says you know what happened to all our parents."

"Hey, let me go!" Sheen cried, switching back to his normal voice.

Cindy Vortex pushed her way through the crowd. "Where's my mom and dad?" she demanded.

When everyone was gathered around, Jimmy activated Goddard's holographic projector. A giant starfield was projected into the sky.

"Long-range sensors picked up these ion trails, showing a departure route for whatever alien species has abducted our parents," Jimmy began.

"As you can see, these trails lead somewhere in the Orion star system, three million light-years away—so we'll need to leave Friday."

The kids began mumbling. "Leave for *where,* exactly?" Cindy asked.

"Wherever the ion trail leads," Jimmy replied. "We have two days to collect the necessary plutonium, design and test our fusion engines, and build our fleet of spaceships."

The kids stared at Jimmy, their mouths hanging open.

"I can get us to the aliens. Then Nick can kick their butts."

"Oh, yeah!" Jimmy cried, smacking his head. "And remember to bring snacks. Any questions?"

"Are you sure about this, Neutron?" asked Nick.

"The data seem to support my hypothesis," he replied.

Sheen nodded. "Never argue with the data."

Everyone looked to Nick Dean. It was up to him to make the final decision. "Let's go get those alien slimeballs!" he cried.

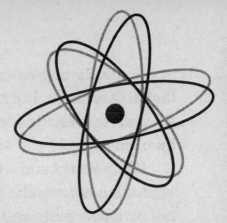

CHAPTER 15

Construction of the space armada began immediately. The Retroland amusement park was transformed into a spaceship assembly site.

The Ferris wheel was used as a crane to reach the tops of the spaceships. The Eye-in-the-Sky ride transported supplies back and forth across the theme park.

Sparks flew from blazing torches at the top of the roller-coaster ride. The tracks would be used as the launching pad.

"Hey, Jimmy! Do these fusion reactors need fuel rods?" asked Sheen.

Jimmy put his hands on his hips. "C'mon, Sheen," he said, "it's not rocket science, you just . . . actually, I guess it *is* rocket science. No fuel rods, Sheen."

From sunup to sundown Jimmy supervised and directed the work. When he was not working at the site, Jimmy was testing materials for space flight. Duct tape, bubblegum, and thumbtacks all had to pass inspection before they could be used to build the spaceships.

Cindy Vortex and Libby were assigned to gather plutonium from the nuclear power plant. They put on safety suits and entered the reactor area. Lights blinked, computers hummed, and electricity crackled. The girls worked in a flourescent glow, carefully loading nuclear material into pedal cars and wagons for delivery. Plutonium would power the Neutron-designed rocket fleet.

When the armada was nearly completed, Jimmy made a final check of the rockets.

"Now for the final touch," he said, slapping a big Neutron bumper sticker on each rocket.

"Good work, everybody," Jimmy declared. "We're ready for intergalactic travel!"

As Jimmy made his way through the crowd Nick grabbed him by his shirt.

"Neutron, this is gonna work, right?"

"Yeah, Jimmy," said Cindy. "What if it doesn't work?"

"It *will* work," Jimmy insisted. "I'm ninety-five percent sure."

"Ninety-five?" Cindy gasped, horrified. "What about the other five percent?"

Jimmy shrugged. "We blow up."

Cindy's eyes grew wide.

"Look, a ninety-five is still an A," Jimmy said.

Nick thought about it. "I can deal with that," he said. "I never got an A in my life."

"You heard the man," Cindy said. "Stop sucking your thumbs, and let's light this candle!"

As the kids raced to their rockets Cindy leaned close to Jimmy.

"If we blow up," she said, "whatever's left of me is going to kick your butt!"

Then Cindy rushed to her rocket for the final countdown.

All over Retroland, kids were buckling themselves into log-shaped cars, into roller-coaster seats, onto merry-go-round horses, and inside ride cages of all shapes and sizes.

Jimmy hopped into his new and improved rocket, the Strato XL, which was perched on a rocket-ride platform. Then he put on his radio headset.

The rocket began to shake as the powerful engine revved up.

"Goddard, initiate launch sequence," Jimmy instructed.

Goddard opened his mouth and his robotic voice boomed. "Please make sure your seat belts are fastened, and remember to keep your hands and arms inside the vehicles at all times. Five . . . four . . . three . . . two . . . one—"

"We have liftoff!" cried Jimmy.

One by one the spaceships leaped into the sky.

Bat-cars flew out of the Bat-out-of-Heck ride in a burst of flame.

The Eye-in-the-Sky shot eyeball-cars out of its sockets, one after the other.

The Viking Ship ride swung back and forth to build momentum, then launched into the air. Kids wearing Viking helmets cheered as the boat lifted off.

The roller-coaster rockets crawled up the first

hill, raced down and up, and then launched from the track.

The Ferris wheel spun faster and faster, rolling across the park like a giant steel tire before lifting off from the ground.

The Octapuke spun in circles until it took off like a flying saucer. The kids aboard were sick before they reached orbit.

The Butterfly ride spun too, faster and faster until the anchor bolts pulled out. In a flurry of flapping wings, the cars lifted off.

All of them but Carl's. His butterfly-car stalled, and its wings didn't flap. Carl spun around and around in circles, getting nowhere.

Carl pounded the controls. "C'mon, butterfly!"

Finally the wings began to move up and down, and Carl's car broke free. He felt the tug of gravity as his butterfly-car accelerated into the air.

Jimmy's rocket lit up and tore away from its launchpad. It arched high over Retroland, leaving a blast of fire in its wake.

The ships flew haphazardly at first.

"Come on, everybody," Jimmy called into his

headset. "Get into formation. Carl, you're too low!"

Carl clung to his seat. "I know! I know! Stupid butterfly."

Sheen was navigating a bat-car. He held on tight as his ship raced through the church belfry, stirring up *real* bats.

Soon the fleet was flying in formation behind the Strato XL. Then Jimmy's control panel began to beep.

"Hang on!" he cried. "We're passing through the stratosphere."

The ships began to shake as they climbed higher and higher.

"Now the mesosphere," Jimmy said.

Carl was jolted up and down in his seat as his butterfly-car flapped wildly. He covered his eyes.

"Strat-os-phere, mes-os-phere . . . now I know why they all end in *f-f-fear*," Carl stammered.

Jimmy patted his rocket. "This is it, baby. Engaging pulse rockets . . . now!"

Just then every rocket in the fleet sputtered and stalled at the exact same time.

"Jimmmmmmmyyyy!!!" Carl howled.

Jimmy looked down. The ground was very far away.

"We're gonna die . . . we're gonna die . . . ," Cindy cried.

Jimmy swallowed hard and closed his eyes, too afraid to look down. He pounded on his control panel. "C'mon, c'mon, c'mon!"

Suddenly there was a mighty roar as the pulse rockets kicked in. In a final fiery burst the space armada blasted free of Earth's atmosphere.

"Yes!" cried Jimmy as the other kids cheered.

"Way to go, Neutron!" said Nick as he leaned back to enjoy the ride.

Far below, the Earth appeared smaller and smaller as the rockets ventured into outer space.

CHAPTER 16

Inside the Yokian marination plant Ooblar was squirting meat tenderizer onto the humans. They stood simmering in bubbling, black soup. As Ooblar worked he sang, "Whizlak, Whizlak, sprinkle, moisten, spray. Dew drop, dew drop, irrigate all day!"

"Ooblar!" King Goobot's voice bellowed through the chamber.

"Y-Y-Yes, sire?"

"You know I despise that song," the king admonished.

"I wasn't aware of your presence," Ooblar cooed. "My gosh, it's an honor."

Ooblar faced the humans.

"All hail the hailee!" he cried, squirting King Goobot with Whizlak. "Care for another?"

"Don't spray me with that thing!" King Goobot yelled.

"But it's good luck," Ooblar insisted.

King Goobot smiled slyly. "Guess what happens if you squirt me again?"

Ooblar thought about it. "Bad luck?"

"Uh-huh," said the king.

"Ah, yes," Ooblar replied. "Ceasing ritual squirt. The purification is going marvelously, Your Blobbatiousness."

King Goobot studied the humans. They stared blankly ahead, still under the control of the Hats of Obedience.

"Oh, I do so hope they put up a good fight for Poultra," said the king.

"Beeekaw! Beeekaw!" Ooblar chanted when he heard Poultra's name.

"Do you think they'll scream?" the king wondered. "I do so love that."

"Oh, yes!" Ooblar said. "They yell out even when merely poked. It's great fun!"

Ooblar swooped over the humans and poked one. "Ow!" the man cried.

"See?" Ooblar said. He flew over the humans, poking them.

"Ow!" Poke. "Ouch!" Poke. "Hey! Watch it!" Poke, poke. "Yikes!" Poke. "Yow!"

"Oh, let me!" the king whined.

King Goobot floated down and poked another human. "Ow!" the man howled.

"This *is* fun!" King Goobot cried as he flew from human to human, giving each one a poke.

"Watch out for the Hats of Obedience," Ooblar cautioned. "Some of them are malfunctioning."

Finally the king reached Mr. Neutron. When he poked Jimmy's dad, Mr. Neutron yelled, "Ouch!"

King Goobot chuckled and moved on to the next human. He didn't notice that the red light on Mr. Neutron's Hat of Obedience flickered green.

※   ※   ※

Meanwhile, Jimmy's fleet raced toward the Orion nebula. Stars gleamed all around them. Comets flashed across the sky.

"The wonders of the universe," Jimmy sighed. "We are witnessing celestial events no person, or dog, has ever seen."

Goddard cooed, clearly impressed.

Cindy flew her ship alongside Jimmy's.

"It's incredible," she said softly.

Cindy and Jimmy stared at each other for a moment, then quickly glanced away.

She turned to Nick, who slouched in the seat of his souped-up bat rocket with big tailfins and furry dice hanging from the rearview mirror. He picked at his nails, bored.

"Beautiful, isn't it, Nick?" asked Cindy.

"Yeah, yeah," Nick said. "Wake me when we get there." He put his rocket on automatic pilot, stretched out, and placed a comic book over his face. Seconds later he was snoring.

Carl zoomed ahead. He squeezed a tube of blue gel into his mouth.

"Hey, this astronaut food isn't bad."

Jimmy winced. "That's toothpaste, Carl."

Carl stared at the tube in his hand. "Mmm. Minty."

Just then a meteor struck Carl's ship, rattling it. Another raced by, just missing it. A third struck Jimmy's rocket, sending the Strato XL into a wild spin.

"Hey! What's happening?" Carl cried.

"Meteor shower!" Jimmy yelled. "Take evasive action immediately!"

A moment later a raging space storm pummeled the fleet. Rocks flew every which way, piercing the rockets and setting off sparks.

Sheen pulled his Ultra Lord mask over his face and slipped into character. "I do so relish these times of peril," he said as he maneuvered his rocket.

"We gotta find shelter!" Jimmy called out.

He checked his control panel. A mass appeared on his radar screen. Something loomed ahead.

"Asteroid!" Jimmy adjusted his radar to get a more accurate fix. "Bearing 236 mark 7 degrees. Follow me!"

CHAPTER 17

The kids waited out the storm on the asteroid. After they built a campfire, Nick told ghost stories.

"So then, the kids are in the woods and they find these sticks shaped like people," Nick said in a creepy voice. "And the girl starts crying, and they don't have *any tissue at all . . .*"

Carl gasped. "None?"

"Then they hear really scary noises and from out of the darkness comes—"

Suddenly a figure burst from the bushes with a startling roar.

"AHHHHHH!" Carl screamed.

The creature had sticks for hair and leaves for a body and . . . and it was really Nick's friend named Benny. "Gotcha!"

"Oh, man," Nick howled. "You should have seen your faces!"

*   *   *

After they ate a meal of vacuum-packed dried beans, the space travelers settled into their sleeping bags for the night. The sky was bright with stars.

"There's a constellation," Jimmy said, pointing. "And that star over there is a red giant, and that other one's a white dwarf."

"You can relate to that one, huh, Neutron?" Nick said.

Cindy and Libby giggled.

Jimmy shook his head and walked away from the group. Carl followed after him.

"What's the matter, Jimmy?" Carl asked.

"Shorty, squirt, small-stuff, shrimp. It gets to you after awhile." Jimmy said with a sigh. "And next year there'll be dances. What girl wants to dance with a guy who comes up to her armpits?"

Carl scratched his head. "I didn't think we liked girls, Jimmy."

"Oh, we don't!" he quickly replied. "Not yet. However, one day an influx of hormones that we can't control will drive us to pursue the female gender against our will."

Carl shivered. "Stop talkin' like that. You're gonna give me nightmares."

Jimmy shrugged. "I wouldn't worry, Carl. I have a feeling that puberty is still light-years away for you and me."

The boys returned to camp just as a shooting star streaked across the night sky.

"You know," Carl whispered sadly. "I should never have wished on that star, 'cause I really miss my folks."

"My mom used to tuck me into bed every night," said Libby.

"Before my dad was abducted by aliens, he used to watch Ultra Lord reruns with me on Saturday mornings," Sheen said.

"Before my mom was abducted by aliens," Carl said, "she would rub my tummy and sing la-la-la . . ."

"What?!" Nick snickered.

"Nothing!" Carl said, blushing. He rolled over and pulled the blanket up to his chin.

The slow crackle of the campfire soon lulled the group to sleep.

CHAPTER 18

The next morning the storm had passed. Everyone boarded the rockets for takeoff. With Jimmy in the lead the rockets streaked through space. Suddenly Goddard began to bark excitedly.

"What is it, boy?"

Goddard leaped onto the nose of Jimmy's rocket and pointed into the distance. A gigantic planet rose into view.

Jimmy sprang into action.

He activated the long-range sensor and studied the data scrolling across his computer screen.

"Sensor sweeps reveal technologically advanced cities and—*ion-energy signatures!*"

Jimmy broadcast the news.

"We've found it! I repeat. We have found it."

Within minutes they entered orbit around the mysterious planet. Jimmy was certain that this was the home of the aliens who had kidnapped their parents.

The spaceships circled around Jimmy's rocket.

"First I'm going to take a search party to make sure the coast is clear," Jimmy said. "We'll contact you as soon as we find the parents. And Nick," Jimmy continued, "get ready to kick the aliens' butts!"

Nick winked. "Piece of cake."

"Okay, scouts, follow me," called Jimmy.

The scouting party included Goddard, Carl, Sheen, Cindy, and Libby. They pulled away from the group and plunged toward the planet below.

❧   ❧   ❧

On the surface of planet Yolkus, Jimmy and his friends marveled at the sights.

There were brightly lit buildings that spiraled high into the clouds. Flying cars formed long lines of aerial traffic.

"Oh, wow!" Jimmy cried when he saw the Yokians floating in their transparent shells. "They've evolved beyond the need for mere conventional bodies. They must be millions of years ahead of us!"

Cindy wrinkled her nose at the gooey green aliens.

"Are you trying to tell me that one day our children's children's children's children could evolve into . . ."

"Snot?" Libby finished.

"Eeeeeeeeeeewwwwww!" The girls cried.

Suddenly Goddard pointed down a crowded Yokian street.

"Grrrrrrr," the robot dog growled.

Jimmy nodded. "Our parents are this way."

※　※　※

Meanwhile, at the royal palace, King Goobot inspected the sacrifices for the festival. Ooblar hovered at Goobot's side while guards stood watch.

The freshly marinated parents were lined up in a holding pen for display. Then they would be loaded onto transports and carried to the arena.

The king floated down the line of humans, poking them once in a while for fun.

"Ooblar, these humans look so scrawny," the

king complained. "Hardly very appetizing. Are you sure they're ready?"

Ooblar darted up and down the line of humans, nodding his head.

"I assure you, my slimy sovereign, the mighty Poultra will—"

"Beeekaw! Beeekaw!" cried the guards.

"—will be quite pleased. The earthlings are mostly water, but with a crunchy, bony center. Think: nuts-and-chews."

"Mmmmm," King Goobot rubbed his shell. "That *does* sound tasty."

🗲 🗲 🗲

Jimmy Neutron's head popped out from behind a statue of the Yokian king.

"There they are," he whispered, pointing to the long line of parents. The others peeked over his shoulder.

"What are they doing?" Carl asked.

Cindy leaned in. "And what are those goofy hats on their heads?"

"It looks like some kind of mind-control device," Jimmy replied.

Then he spotted his mom and dad.

"Mom! Dad! It's me, Jimmy! Over here!"

The light on Mr. Neutron's Hat of Obedience flickered from red to green. Jimmy's dad looked around, confused. Then he saw his son.

"Jimmy!" he cried. "Jimmy, Jimmy, James, Jim, Jimbo, Jim-Jim, Jimmy!" he babbled excitedly. "Some dream, huh? 'Attack of the Slimy Egg People.'"

"Shhhhh!" Jimmy whispered, glancing at the Yokian guards. "We came to rescue you."

Then Mr. Neutron saw Mrs. Neutron. She stared blankly into the distance.

"Judy?!" He cried, waving his arms in front of her face. "Something's wrong with your mother, Jimmy!"

Mr. Neutron reached up to remove his hat. But when he touched it, a flashing light popped out of the Hat of Obedience and a loud alarm began to sound. Mr. Neutron reverted to his zombielike state.

"Intruder alert! Intruder alert!" he said in a robotic voice.

"Your dad is ratting us out!" Sheen cried.

Jimmy tried to cover his father's mouth. But Mr. Neutron wouldn't be quieted.

"Let's get out of here!" Jimmy yelled. "And fast!"

But just as Jimmy and his friends turned to run, doors opened and hundreds of Yokian guards rushed in, surrounding them with energy spears.

CHAPTER 19

"Well, well," King Goobot chuckled. "If it isn't the littlest rescue party. He reached down and tickled Cindy under her chin. "Hello, itty-bitty human!"

"Let us go, you big ball of phlegm!" Cindy cried as she struggled against the guards.

Ooblar hovered over the girl. "That's *royal* ball of phlegm to you."

Jimmy pulled away from a Yokian guard and stepped forward.

"I think it's only fair to warn you that an army of highly trained combat specialists is on course to destroy your entire planet!" he said.

"Oh, really?" King Goobot cooed.

"Really."

"Oh, my!" the king cried in mock terror. "Whatever shall we do? Please have mercy on us, teeny human with the not-so-teeny head."

King Goobot grinned evilly.

"Do you mean *this* army of highly trained combat specialists?"

A huge door swung open, revealing Nick Dean and the rest of the kids. Nick struggled in the grip of a Yokian guard. "Get your grubs off me, you pus wad!"

"Don't look so surprised, little earthlings," King Goobot said. "We're an advanced alien race. What did you expect?"

"What do you want with our parents?" Libby demanded.

"It's not what *I* want," King Goobot replied. "It's what *Poultra* wants. . . ."

"Beeekaw! Beeekaw! Beeekaw!" the guards chanted.

Cindy blinked. "Who's Poultra?"

"Beeekaw! Beeekaw! Beeekaw!" said the guards.

King Goobot raised a finger. "Poultra—"

"Beeekaw! Beeekaw! Beeekaw!"

The Yokian king glared at the palace guards.

"Poultra is our god," the king continued. "The mightiest, most ferocious creature in all of—oh, I get tired of answering this question."

The king picked up a remote control. "Here," he said, "just watch the movie."

A giant television descended from the ceiling. With the touch of a button, two Yokian newsanchors appeared on the screen.

"Hello, and welcome to our special edition of *Poultra: God of Wrath*," said one announcer. "This show is brought to you by—"

King Goobot hit the FAST-FORWARD button.

"Commercials," he muttered. "Hate them."

"Welcome back!" the anchor continued. "If you are watching this, chances are your friends and/or relatives are about to be sacrificed to the mighty Poultra—a great honor indeed!"

The picture changed from brilliant color to grainy black-and-white. A primitive Yokian village appeared.

"In days of yore, Poultra terrorized innocent Yokians with his yearly rampages through our humble villages."

The shadow of a gigantic creature fell over the village. Giant, scaly feet appeared, crushing the huts and scattering the fearful Yokians.

"But ever since our high priests instituted

annual sacrifices, Poultra's savage attacks are a thing of the past!"

On the screen a strange-looking alien cowered in fear. A moment later a gigantic creature swooped down and gobbled him in a single gulp. Jimmy and his friends turned away.

The scene switched back to the two anchors.

"And this year's sacrifices feature something very special. Humans! And it's all thanks to little Jimmy Neutron!" the Yokian announcer said.

The kids stared at Jimmy, shocked and confused.

Then the video of Jimmy's satellite message appeared. Jimmy's face filled the screen.

"Greetings from planet Earth! I'm Jimmy Neutron. I welcome the opportunity to meet with you for the mutual exchange of scientific knowledge and universal brotherhood . . . ," the TV image of Jimmy said.

King Goobot sneered. "You see, Jimmy, without the coordinates you gave us, we never would have found your little planet. For such a tiny earthling, you've been a very big help!"

King Goobot turned to his guards.

"Throw these minuscule vermin into the dungeon until they are of worthier size. And give Jimmy Neutron the presidential suite!"

But as the guards dragged the kids away, Goddard jumped into their path.

"Bark! Bark! Grrrrrrrr," the robot dog growled.

King Goobot picked up the struggling pooch. "Oooooh!" he gushed. "Isn't this a funny little toy?"

Goddard sunk his steel teeth into King Goobot's arm. The king howled and jumped around, but he could not shake the robot dog loose.

"Get it off me! Get it off me!" he cried.

Finally the guards managed to tear Goddard off the king.

"Take this infernal thing to the lab and have it dissected," demanded the king.

"NOOOOO!" Jimmy screamed.

CHAPTER 20

Jimmy and his friends were locked in a dungeon beneath the palace.

"So it was Neutron all along," Nick Dean said. "*He* got us into this mess."

Nick's voice echoed against the stone walls of the underground prison. Jimmy cringed in his nearby cell.

"Hey, Jimmy?" Libby called out. "Didn't your parents ever tell you not to talk to strangers. That's Rule Number One!"

"Come on, you guys," Cindy said. "Give him a break." Then her voice got sarcastic. "Jimmy didn't mean to ruin our lives and get our parents eaten by a giant space monster."

"She's right," Sheen said. "We should ask ourselves, 'what would Ultra Lord do?'"

"Oh, yeah, let's think about *that,* why don't we?" Nick replied. "Maybe Ultra Lord would just sit on a shelf because he's a DOLL!"

"He's not a doll!" Sheen cried. "He's an *action figure!*"

"Come on, Nick," Carl said. "Let Sheen finish. Maybe he's on to something. What would Ultra Lord do, Sheen?"

"Well," Sheen replied, "in episode 224 he fried the Zeebots' brains with his heat-seeking infra-thought."

"Well, I'm convinced," Nick told the others. "That's pretty much *the stupidest thing I've ever heard!*"

"You're just picking on me because you're insecure," Sheen muttered.

Nick snorted. "Whatever, Ultra Dork. I'm cool. Something you and your friend Jimmy will never be. . . ."

"Leave Sheen alone!" Carl demanded.

"Okay, then I'll pick on you!"

Soon everyone was bickering.

Cindy turned away from the argument. "Jimmy?" she called from her cell. "Jimmy? Can you hear me?"

In the darkness Cindy saw Jimmy huddled on the floor in the corner of his cell. "I'm sorry

I gave you a hard time. We're all just scared," she said. Cindy listened for a long time, but Jimmy didn't reply. "Are you okay?"

Jimmy sniffed back a tear. "Yeah. I'm fine."

"Don't be so hard on yourself," she said. "We'll get out of this."

Jimmy was silent.

Cindy sat down next to the bars. "You know," she said, "I was the smartest kid in school until you came along. And I admit you know more about some things than I do. But I know one thing that you don't seem to get."

Jimmy sat up.

"We're never getting out of here without you, Jimmy. So buck up, mister, and put that big brain of yours to work. Nick can handle the fighting stuff, but first we have to get out of this dungeon."

"Uh . . . Cindy," Jimmy said in a low voice, "why are you being so nice to me?"

Cindy sighed. "Because there's a bunch of kids in here that need you." She paused. "And I need you too."

Meanwhile, Carl scurried away from a furry green spider that was crawling toward him. He looked up and saw a skeleton with six arms.

"AHHH!" he screamed. "I am *never* complaining about my parents again!"

"We didn't even get our one phone call," Nick Dean cried.

Jimmy Neutron sprang to his feet.

"That's it!" Jimmy cried. "Libby, let me use your cell phone!"

"Okay," she said, handing it through the bars. "But I don't think my service plan covers anything outside our solar system."

"This is a *local* call," Jimmy replied.

*   *   *

In another part of the royal palace, inside a secret laboratory, Ooblar tinkered with Jimmy Neutron's robot dog. Goddard rolled from side to side, trying to wiggle off the table.

"You really must not delay the inevitable," Ooblar insisted.

He jammed a screwdriver into Goddard's neck and unscrewed a bolt.

Suddenly Ooblar jumped backward, surprised. Goddard was *ringing.*

"C'mon, boy, pick up," Jimmy said into the cell phone.

"Bark!" Goddard replied.

Jimmy smiled. "You're okay!"

"Bark! Bark!"

"I miss you too, boy," Jimmy said. "What's your situation?"

In a secret language known only to Jimmy and Goddard, the robotic dog explained what was going on.

"Don't worry," Jimmy said. "I've got an idea. Put me on speakerphone!"

"Bark!" said Goddard.

Ooblar pulled open a small panel in Goddard's stomach. A loud voice rang out.

"Danger! Danger! You have initiated self-destruct sequence," Jimmy said in a robotic voice.

"Ooh! That's not good," Ooblar said.

He closed the panel and screwed it in place.

"Self-destruct sequence is now engaged."

"No, no, no!" Ooblar cried, frantically. "I closed the panel! Don't self-destruct!"

"This unit will yield a fifty-megaton nuclear blast in exactly ten seconds. . . ."

"That's really not good," said Ooblar.

"Please clear a thirty-square-mile area. Thank you, and have a nice day. . . ."

"Bad dog! Please stop!" Ooblar pleaded.

"Ten . . . nine . . . eight . . . seven . . ."

Ooblar ran out of the lab screaming.

Goddard barked twice.

"He's gone? Good boy!" Jimmy replied. "Now, lock on to this signal and get here as fast as you can!"

Goddard scampered out of the lab and through the corridors until he reached the entrance to the dungeon. At the gate Goddard ran right into a Yokian guard.

"Halt! Who goes there?" the guard demanded.

"Bark! Bark! Bark! Bark!" Goddard replied. Then he charged the Yokian.

The guard raised his spear.

"By order of the most esteemed King Goobot, it is my great privilege to exterminate you!"

"Goddard!" Jimmy yelled. "Play dead!" Then Jimmy covered his ears.

BOOM!

When Goddard blew up, the explosion rocked the entire dungeon. The guard screamed as his shell shattered. Now a puddle of green goo, the Yokian sloshed onto the floor.

The blast was so powerful it shattered the door to Jimmy's cell.

Through the smoke and haze Jimmy watched Goddard reassemble himself. Goddard picked up the guard's keys in his mouth and ran to Jimmy.

"Let's get the others!"

Jimmy unlocked the cell and freed the other kids. Cindy Vortex was the first one out. She looked down at the gooey puddle at her feet that was once the Yokian guard. Then she turned to Jimmy.

"If you ever tell anyone I was nice to you, I'll . . . I'll . . ."—she pointed at the pool of slime—"I'll make sure you wind up looking like that guy!"

CHAPTER 21

The Yokian festival arena was sold out. Thousands of Yokians jammed into the stadium to watch the annual celebration. They sat shell-to-shell, waving banners and cheering. Vendors moved through the crowd, selling snacks and souvenirs.

In the center of the arena an enormous egg was perched on a platform. The egg was surrounded by dozens of microwave dishes. When the king gave the sign, the dishes would heat up and hatch the egg.

A spotlight hit the stage.

"Welcome to the two-billion and twenty-third annual Festival of Poultra!" the Yokian announcer began.

"Tonight, direct from planet Earth, a sacrificial harvest guaranteed to please the mighty Poultra!"

"Beeekaw! Beeekaw! Beeekaw!" chanted the crowd.

"Thus providing us with many cycles of good fortune. And how many of us couldn't use that?"

High up in the royal box-seats King Goobot arrived with Ooblar in tow.

"Ooblar?" said the king. "Did you dispose of that infernal puppy?"

"What? Oh, of course, sire," Ooblar lied. "I . . . uh . . . disposed the living daylights out of him."

Suddenly a transport ship appeared over the arena. The crowd went wild.

Outside the stadium a shadow fell over Jimmy and his friends as the transport ship moved into position.

"Our parents must be in there," Jimmy pointed. "Remember the plan. Nick goes in first and kicks the aliens' butts."

With a cloud of smoke the transport ship landed in the arena. Doors opened and the parents marched out of the ship like zombies.

King Goobot rose and addressed the crowd.

"My fellow Yokians, this is the moment

we've been waiting for. The sacrifice that will bring good fortune and prosperity to us all. . . ."

The king paused as the crowd erupted in cheers.

"Let us unite in praise of the great and mighty Poultra!"

"Beeekaw! Beeekaw! Beeekaw!"

King Goobot held up his hand. "Begin the incubation!" he cried.

The microwave dishes surrounding the egg began to glow, bathing the egg in red light. After a few seconds a crack appeared in the egg's smooth surface.

The crowd gasped.

"Lookie, lookie," Ooblar gushed. "There it is!"

Then the high priest began to sing. "Oh, the first crack I see . . . is good luck for me!"

"Ooblar?"

"Yes, sire?"

The king towered over him. "Put a sock in it."

"Certainly, sire," Ooblar replied, nodding quickly. "But, sire? What is a sock?"

Just then a massive beak broke through the shell. When a second crack appeared, a hush fell over the crowd.

A giant, scaly leg burst through. Then another. The legs lifted the egg into the air as the creature—still in its shell—stomped on the stage. Its massive bulk shook the whole stadium.

Meanwhile, Jimmy and his friends raced through a tunnel toward the stadium floor.

Nick Dean took the lead. "Nobody eats my parents unless I say so!" he cried.

"Go get 'em, Nick!" cheered Cindy.

Just as Nick ran out of the tunnel, Poultra burst out of his shell. The monstrous chicken's head rose until it towered over the crowd. Poultra scanned the arena with three beady eyes and then let out a horrid cry:

"BEEEKAW! BEEEKAW! BE-BE-BEEEKAW!"

Nick froze in his tracks. When the monster turned toward him, Nick ran screaming back into the tunnel.

His retreat caused panic among the kids as they scrambled for cover. Only Jimmy Neutron held his ground.

"Nick!" he cried. "Come back!"

But Nick Dean was long gone. And so was everyone else.

❋ ❋ ❋

King Goobot motioned to the royal DJ. "Kick it!" he commanded.

The disk jockey popped a CD into a slot in his shell. Strange, hypnotic music filled the arena. A forcefield rose up around Poultra, trapping the predatory chicken on the stage.

When they heard the music, the parents were made to dance in honor of Poultra. At first all the adults swayed to the music. But soon the thoughts and memories from their youth took over, and the dance changed. Some of the parents danced the fox-trot, others the twist. A few adults began to break-dance. They spun across the stage, twirling on their Hats of Obedience.

Jimmy's parents danced the funky chicken, flailing their arms around like wings.

Back in the tunnel Jimmy found Nick cowering in a corner.

"Nick didn't kick their butts!" Carl cried. "What do we do now?"

"We need another plan," Sheen declared. "But this plan has got to be Nickless."

Libby peeked around the corner of the tunnel entrance and gasped. Inside the arena Poultra opened his gigantic mouth to reveal massive, pointy teeth. He drooled with hunger as he watched the dancing humans.

"Poultra's about to eat our parents!" Libby cried.

"Somebody think of something fast," Carl moaned.

"Goddard, Bino-scope mode!" said Jimmy.

Goddard's head instantly turned into a combination of binoculars and a periscope. Jimmy grabbed the ears like handgrips as Goddard's eyes became lenses.

Jimmy surveyed the stadium. He spotted the control booth with the joystick that controlled the Hats of Obedience.

He also saw an airfield in the distance.

"Okay, think, think, think . . . ," Jimmy muttered, pacing back and forth.

"Are you feeling okay?" asked Libby.

"A-okay!" Jimmy replied. He turned to Sheen.

"There's an airfield about a mile to the north. I need you to secure a transport ship and get it to the arena. We're counting on you, buddy."

Sheen pulled his Ultra Lord mask over his

face and then strode away purposefully.

Jimmy turned to the others.

"There's a joystick in the tower that controls our parents," he said. "I'm going after it. I'll send up a flare as soon as I have control."

Jimmy turned to the girls.

"Cindy, you take some of the others and try to distract Poultra. Libby, get to those incubator rays and start frying some egg!"

"What do I do, Jimmy?" asked Carl.

Jimmy cringed. "Uh . . . you're the secret weapon. Just try not to get hurt."

Jimmy Neutron addressed the group.

"These gooballs stole our parents. We've gotta show them what we're made of! We're tough! We're unruly! We're unpredictable! And, darn it, we're carbon-based life-forms!"

Jimmy smiled. "Now, who's ready to kick some alien butt?"

CHAPTER 22

While the parents continued to dance, Poultra lunged at them hungrily. But the forcefield prevented the deity from feasting—for now.

"When the music stops, the forcefield drops," sang Ooblar. "And the earthlings are gobbled up like gumdrops!"

Inside the control booth a Yokian technician worked the joystick that made the parents dance. He snickered as he jiggled the controls.

Then the Yokian felt a tap on his shell. He turned to find another Yokian standing behind him . . . or so the Yokian thought.

Jimmy and Goddard sat inside a Yokian shell that they had found discarded behind the stadium.

"Break time!" Jimmy said in a Yokian voice.

"Already? Praise Poultra!" the technician said.

"Beeekaw!!!" Jimmy cried.

When the technician flew away, Jimmy took control of the joystick.

※　※　※

Down in the arena the music stopped and the forcefield vanished.

Poultra opened his beak and reared back, ready to devour the sacrifices.

But before Poultra had a chance to pluck one, the parents stopped dancing and ran.

"What, what, what?!" King Goobot cried. "What are those humans doing?"

King Goobot looked up at the control booth. Jimmy Neutron waved and wiggled the control so all the parents waved too.

"The Earth brats!" King Goobot howled. "Neutron thinks he's had the last laugh, but he's wrong."

"Well, it *is* kind of funny, Your Highness," said Ooblar.

"Oh, yes," said the king. "Very funny. Very funny indeed. About as funny as . . . the Doomstick!"

And with that, King Goobot tapped Ooblar

with the Doomstick, and Ooblar spilled onto the ground in a puddle of gooey yolk.

"Now, Goddard!" Jimmy said. The dog barked, then fired an atomic flare that exploded in a blast of color.

"Jimmy's signal!" Cindy cried. "Come on, people, let's wreak *havoc!*"

The kids raced down the tunnel and into the arena.

"Alert the troops!" King Goobot cried.

A battalion of Yokian guards raced to the arena floor. They drove the kids back with energy spears. One guard landed in front of Carl, spear raised.

"Carl!" Jimmy called. "Remember show-and-tell?"

Carl nodded. He fumbled in his pocket and pulled out his inhaler.

"You want a piece of me?!" Carl cried. Then he tipped the Yokian's shell open and squirted his inhaler right into the guard's eyes.

"I can't see! I can't see!" screamed the hapless Yokian. He stumbled into two more guards and their shells cracked open, spilling green yolk onto the floor.

Carl twirled his inhaler and pocketed it like a six-shooter.

Meanwhile, a Yokian cornered Cindy Vortex.

"Dragon whips her tail, hah!" She finished him off with her favorite Tai Chi move.

Another guard aimed his energy spear at Cindy. Jimmy swooped down and cracked the guard in half.

"For a nerd, you sure come in handy," Cindy said.

A guard grabbed Jimmy. He was just about to pounce when Carl leaped in front with his inhaler.

"Squirt! Squirt! Take that!" he yelled.

Libby jumped behind the incubator controls.

"Let's dance!" she cried, aiming the heat ray at the Yokians. She pulled the trigger and blasted them into hard-boiled eggs.

Jimmy spied the exit. "Now's our chance! Let's go!"

The kids hurried their parents along.

"Beeekaw! Beeekaw! Beeekaw!" Poultra raged.

"Yes, Poultra!" King Goobot bellowed. "Eat them! Eat them all!"

126

Poultra's massive claw slammed down, blocking the exit.

"Roadblock," Cindy warned.

"Beeekaw!" Poultra roared, spotting Jimmy.

"Cindy, get our parents out of here!" Jimmy cried. Then he waved his arms at Poultra.

"Hey, you big chicken!" Jimmy yelled. "Come and get me!"

"Beeekaw!"

Poultra stomped across the arena and loomed over Jimmy, snapping his beak angrily.

"Jimmy! Look out!" cried Cindy.

CHAPTER 23

Sheen crept into the busy spaceport hangar and ducked behind a pile of boxes just as a Yokian pilot flew overhead.

When the Yokian was gone, Sheen cautiously peeked above the cargo boxes.

Chicken-ships were parked everywhere. Yokians buzzed around, busy with their duties. Sheen spied a large space freighter parked away from the other ships.

"Ah, a worthy vessel," he said.

Keeping to the shadows, Sheen made it to the freighter. A Yokian pilot was unlocking the hatch with a card-key.

Sheen pulled his Ultra Lord visor over his face.

"That's far enough, alien!" he commanded.

"Oh, my!" the Yokian pilot said with a chuckle.

"Ultra Lord, activate Firing Fists!"

Sheen's small fists bounced off the pilot's

transparent shell with a hollow *thunk.*

"My hands! My hands!" the boy howled.

"Oh, you got me!" the Yokian said, still laughing.

Then a tiny crack appeared in the Yokian's shell. And another. His shell burst and he splashed to the tarmac. Sheen unlocked the hatch and boarded the vessel.

❉   ❉   ❉

Just as Poultra was about to snatch Jimmy up and swallow him whole, the transport ship burst through the arena wall, knocking Poultra aside.

CRASH! Poultra's beak struck the ground, barely missing Jimmy, and got stuck.

Sheen navigated the ship to the ground. "Your ship awaits, Captain Jimmy," he said. "Everybody to the ship!" Jimmy cried out.

Just as the hatch door closed behind them, Poultra's beak broke free and the creature lunged at the ship. "Beeekaw! Beeekaw!"

Jimmy jumped into the pilot seat. "Ten, nine, eight . . ." The ground shook as the transport ship blasted off.

CHAPTER 24

King Goobot watched angrily as the spaceship took off.

"Ooblar! Pick up the pace!" he demanded.

"Yes, sire. Right away!" Ooblar cried. He oozed along behind the king as fast as he could go—which wasn't very fast at all.

"Never mind," the king said as he scooped Ooblar into a bucket. Then he turned to Poultra. "How could you let them get away? You big, stupid, slow moving . . ."

Poultra moved toward the king. He eyed him hungrily. "Beeekaw!"

"Uh . . . d-d-don't worry, O mighty one, I'll get your dinner back," King Goobot said. "To the ships!"

🌟 🌟 🌟

Inside the cockpit of the Yokian space

freighter Jimmy wrestled for control as the ship spun in circles. Goddard, ears back, barked and barked.

Cindy sat next to Jimmy in the copilot's chair. "How do you know what to do?" she asked.

"Does it look like I know what to do?" he replied.

Through the window Jimmy saw the entire chicken-ship armada in close pursuit. The Yokian warships fired their payload of missiles. Jimmy worked the controls, dodging the first deadly volley.

But more missiles were on the way.

"Uh . . . Jimmy!" cried Carl. "Here they come!"

"I see 'em," Jimmy said. Suddenly his radar scanner beeped and a warning appeared on the screen:

PLANETOID AHEAD.

Jimmy swallowed hard. "Hang on, everyone."

He zoomed around the planetoid, trying to get behind the Yokians. But when Jimmy peeked over his shoulder, the armada was still following.

"This freighter is too slow!"

"Oh, no! Oh, no!" Carl stammered. "They're getting closer."

The radar scanner beeped again:

SWISS ASTEROID AHEAD.

"Hmmm," said Jimmy. "That might work."

Jimmy plunged the space freighter into one of the many holes that pitted the Swiss asteroid's cheeselike surface.

Racing through a maze of narrow tunnels Jimmy watched as two Yokian ships slammed into each other.

When they spotted Jimmy's freighter, the chicken-ships fired again. The missiles bounced around inside the cavernous tunnels in the asteroid and blew up other Yokian ships.

"The guys at the office will never believe this one!" Mr. Neutron cried.

� ✴ ✴

Inside the Yokian flagship King Goobot was hopping mad.

"Oh, look out! Turn left!" he cried as his vessel barely missed another exploding chicken-ship.

"Could you tell me what's happening?" Ooblar whined. "I can't see out of this bucket." He sloshed against the sides, trying to get a look.

With missles flying all around, Jimmy knew

it was only a matter of time before they would be hit.

"Let's get out of here!"

Jimmy guided his spaceship to the nearest exit hole as one of the Yokian ships fired another volley of missiles at them.

"Cover your ears!" Jimmy warned.

KAAAA-BOOOOM!

Jimmy's ship streaked out of the Swiss asteroid just as it exploded! The blast was so powerful it blew up the Swiss asteroid and the rest of the chicken armada still inside of it.

Suddenly the freighter was rocked by another explosion. Someone had fired at them.

Outside the window the Yokian flagship emerged from the cloud of smoke and debris.

"I want to go home, I want to go home, I want to go home," Nick repeated, covering his eyes.

King Goobot's voice crackled over the radio. "You can't win, Jimmy Neutron!" King Goobot cried. "Fire everything!"

Hundreds of guns popped out of the Yokian flagship. They were all pointed at Jimmy's space freighter.

"This ends now," said Jimmy. "Cindy, take the controls."

"What are you going to do?" Cindy asked.

But Jimmy and his dog were already gone.

CHAPTER 25

"Fly-cycle mode, Goddard!"

Jimmy Neutron burst from the space freighter's cargo hold, riding his dog like a flying motorcycle.

They raced toward the Yokian warship. With a determined look on his face, Jimmy skidded to a halt in the path of the enormous Yokian vessel.

"Well, well," King Goobot said, rubbing his hands together. "Looks like you decided to play chicken with the wrong breed!"

The Yokian ship surged forward, but Jimmy refused to budge.

"You stole my parents. You messed with my dog. You scared my friends. And you made fun of my size!" he cried.

Jimmy pulled the shrink-ray gun out of his pocket. "I may be small," he said, "but I've got a very BIG brain!"

135

Jimmy aimed the shrink ray at himself and flipped the REVERSE switch. Instantly he and Goddard were enlarged to the size of a planet.

Ooblar peeked over the side of his bucket long enough to see Jimmy Neutron's face fill the window.

"Look out!" he screamed.

The Yokian warship screeched to a halt. Jimmy peered at the cowering Yokians.

"Can't we just call this whole thing a mistake and go back to your plan," King Goobot pleaded. "You know, universal brotherhood and whatnot?"

Jimmy took a deep breath and blew as hard as he could.

The Yokian flagship was tossed like a leaf in a windstorm. It spun madly out of control and exploded against an asteroid.

Floating helplessly in space as a puddle of yolk, King Goobot shook his fists at the boy genius.

"You've not seen the last of us, Jimmy Neutron!" he vowed.

As Jimmy raced past the defeated king the

rocket blast from his Fly-cycle fried Ooblar and King Goobot.

Jimmy looked back over his shoulder. "Just the way I like my eggs," Jimmy cried. "Fried!"

※　※　※

The invasion finally over, parents and kids were reunited inside the freighter hold. Nick threw himself into his mom's arms. Then Mrs. Dean saw the smiley-skull tattoo on Nick's arm.

"That's coming off right now, young man," she said, licking her finger and rubbing it away.

Carl was engulfed in his parents' arms. "Can we go for ice cream when we get home?" he asked.

"Mom, Dad," Jimmy said, "I should have listened to you when you said not to talk to strangers. I guess I thought I was smart enough to do everything on my own. But I was wrong. Really wrong."

Mrs. Neutron hugged Jimmy.

"We don't like telling you no all the time, Jimmy. We only do what we do—"

"Because you love me," Jimmy finished, hugging his mom back.

"Exactly," Mr. Neutron said with a smile. "Having a ten-year-old genius for a son may not always be easy, but it's always interesting."

❈   ❈   ❈

A few days later things were back to normal in Retroville. Carl stopped by Jimmy's house for breakfast before they went to Retroland.

"Here you are, gentlemen," Mrs. Neutron said, placing two plates in front of them. "Eggs. Fried, just the way you like them."

Jimmy and Carl stared at their plates. Carl's face turned green.

"Oh, and Jimmy," Mrs. Neutron added as she left the kitchen, "remember you promised to mow the lawn today."

Carl stuck his fork in an egg and watched the yolk ooze. He drank his milk instead.

"Hey," he said between gulps, "did you really destroy all of those mind-control hats?"

Jimmy Neutron smirked.

"Well, I kept one . . . for research. Strictly for research."

Jimmy motioned out the window just as Mr. Neutron passed by, eyes glazed over, pushing the lawnmower. Goddard barked and chased after him. On his head blinked the Hat of Obedience.

Just then Mrs. Neutron noticed her husband outside. She shook her head in disbelief. "James Isaac Neutron!"

EPILOGUE

Back at Retroville Elementary School another epic battle was coming to a close.

Mrs. Fowl brandished her toothpick like a sword. Using it to drive back the monstrous worm, she wrapped a rubber band around its head. Then she hopped aboard, riding on the creature's back. She pointed her toothpick toward the exit.

"Onward, to the cafeteria!" she cried triumphantly.

ABOUT THE AUTHOR

Marc Cerasini has written many books for children, including books based on *Star Wars Episode I* and a series of original Godzilla adventures. He is also the author of the best-selling biography of Princess Diana, *Diana, Queen of Hearts,* and coauthor of the The *Official Godzilla Compendium.* Marc lives in New York City with his wife, Alice, his two cats, Brownie and Turtle, and an impressive collection of action figures.